THE TRAITOR'S BLADE

Also by Kevin Sands

The Blackthorn Key
Mark of the Plague
The Assassin's Curse
Call of the Wraith

THE BLACKTHORN KEY

THE TRAITOR'S BLADE

BOOK 5

KEVIN SANDS

ALADDIN

NEW YORK   LONDON   TORONTO   SYDNEY   NEW DELHI

ALADDIN

An imprint of Simon & Schuster Children's Publishing Division
1230 Avenue of the Americas, New York, New York 10020
First Aladdin hardcover edition May 2021
Text copyright © 2021 by Kevin Sands
Interior illustrations on pages 56, 58, 65, 101, 196, 204, 212, 256, 374
copyright © 2021 by Jim Madsen
Sir Erkenwald's tomb image on page 180 courtesy of
Hathi Trust Digital Library (public domain)
Whitehall 1860 map image on pages 55 and 283 courtesy of
Wikimedia Commons (public domain)
Jacket illustration and interior illustrations on pages 167–171
copyright © 2021 by James Fraser
For information about special discounts for bulk purchases, please contact Simon & Schuster
Special Sales at 1-866-506-1949 or business@simonandschuster.com.
The Simon & Schuster Speakers Bureau can bring authors to your live event. For more
information or to book an event contact the Simon & Schuster Speakers Bureau at
1-866-248-3049 or visit our website at www.simonspeakers.com.
Series design by Karin Paprocki
Jacket designed by Karin Paprocki
Interior designed by Hilary Zarycky
The text of this book was set in Adobe Garamond Pro.
Manufactured in the United States of America 0421 FFG
2 4 6 8 10 9 7 5 3 1
Library of Congress Cataloging-in-Publication Data
Names: Sands, Kevin, author.
Title: The traitor's blade / by Kevin Sands.
Description: First Aladdin hardcover edition. | New York : Aladdin, 2021. |
Series: The blackthorn key | Summary: In 1666, after four months away, friends Christopher
Rowe, Tom, and Sally return to London triumphantly but, guided by coded riddles, face a
conspiracy that threatens Christopher, as well as the king himself.
Identifiers: LCCN 2020040952 (print) | LCCN 2020040953 (eBook)
ISBN 9781534484566 (hardcover) | ISBN 9781534484580 (eBook)
Subjects: CYAC: Adventure and adventurers—Fiction. | Ciphers—Fiction. | Apprentices—
Fiction. | Friendship—Fiction. | Secret societies—Fiction. | London—History—17th
century—Fiction. | Great Britain—History—Charles II, 1660–1685—Fiction.
Classification: LCC PZ7.1.S26 Tr 2021 (print) | LCC PZ7.1.S26 (eBook) | DDC [Fic]—dc23
LC record available at https://lccn.loc.gov/2020040952
LC eBook record available at https://lccn.loc.gov/2020040953

WEDNESDAY, MARCH 3, 1666

Fair is foul, and foul is fair.

CHAPTER

1

"IT WAS AN ACCIDENT," I SAID.

The carriage burned with a bright orange flame. Fire raged across its body, the silk curtains fluttering through the windows in smoking tatters to the road. The frame turned charcoal black, while inside, the stuffing in the seats gave bright flashing bursts as buttons popped off the upholstery.

Tom clutched his cheeks in horror. "I told you," he said, staring at the slowly crumpling carriage, our boots sinking in the mud. "I told you."

The heat drove away the late winter's chill, but I wouldn't have felt it anyway. My face was burning with shame. "It was an accident."

"I *told* you."

Sally stood next to him with her head bowed, palm covering her eyes, auburn curls falling across her face. I'd never seen her so disappointed. "Oh, Christopher."

Behind us, a farmer, his wife, and two young daughters leaned against a wooden fence, cattle watching nervously from a distance. The girls gawked in wide-eyed amazement. Their father, chewing absently on a piece of straw, considered the flames.

"Now there's a thing I never seen before," he said.

"It was an accident," I said.

He nodded. "Would almost have to be."

Ahead of us, twenty of the King's Men waited, stunned, atop their warhorses. A pair of them had dismounted and were now soothing the four draft horses they'd cut loose from our carriage. The road smelled like smoke and cows.

Tom moaned. "Why wouldn't you listen? Why? Just another couple hours and we'd be back in London in a nice dry room, meeting the king. And everyone would be happy, and we could say, 'An honor to see you again, Your Majesty,' instead of 'Goodness, Your Majesty, I hope you didn't want your carriage back, because it's sort of on fire!'"

Sally shook her head. "Oh, *Christopher*."

I didn't have time to answer. The leader of our band had arrived. Riding ahead of our escort, he'd come back when he saw his men had stopped outside this farm. Or, more probably, when he saw the king's carriage burning in front of the supply wagons.

Slowly, the man maneuvered his mount through the mud. His horse, a veteran of many battles, seemed unfazed by the bonfire.

Lord Ashcombe, the King's Warden, dismounted. He was dressed, as usual, in black, wearing fur to keep out the cold. An embroidered patch covered his left eye, an angry scar tracing from under it to the side of his mouth, which turned upward in a permanent half scowl. His pearl-handled pistols, polished to a fine sheen, hung off his belt, grips forward.

He regarded the carriage for a moment. Then he grabbed me by the collar and pulled me close.

His voice was like gravel. *"Explain."*

"It was an accident," I said.

He looked like he was ready to add me to the blaze. I spoke quickly.

"Right . . . um . . . well . . . Tom and I were talking, and . . . and I said wouldn't it be amazing if . . . if you could mount a cannon on a carriage? And fire it."

"Ridiculous," Lord Ashcombe said. "The recoil would flip it like a leaf."

"Well, yes. Tom said that. But then it occurred to me: What if you had *two* cannons? One on either side. So you could fire both at the same time. And make the carriage of steel, instead of wood, so it wouldn't crumple. Then you could ride your carriage into the enemy and shoot it off. Like a warship, but on land. A mobile artillery platform."

Lord Ashcombe looked off into the distance. "A mobile artillery platform . . . ," he mused. Then he blinked. "Why am I considering this?"

His grip tightened. For someone who only had three fingers on his right hand, he sure was strong. I almost told him he was strangling me, but then I supposed that was the point.

I continued. "Anyway—ergh—we didn't have cannons, obviously, but . . . well, you know those fireworks I made last night? To celebrate the fact we'd finally be back in London today? I remembered I had one left in my apothecary sash."

Actually, I had three left. But I didn't think it wise to mention that.

"So . . . er . . . I told Tom it wouldn't need to be a

cannon. We could shoot rockets at our enemies. Call it Blackthorn's Fire-Spitter! And . . . well, never mind. Anyway, I said I'd show him."

Tom tried to shrink into the mud. Seeing as how he was about three times my size, he wasn't particularly successful.

I did try to get him out of trouble. "Now, Tom said this was a bad idea, he did. But I thought, how can research be a bad idea? You always learn something, even when you fail. That's what Master Benedict said."

That was sort of true. I mean, my late master *had* said that—though it hadn't stopped me getting punished from time to time. "Anyway, I tied the firework to a stick and lit it. It was supposed to shoot into the meadow. But . . . well . . . the road was so *bumpy*. I . . . might have lost control of it. Just for a second."

Sometimes it's the second that counts. Lord Ashcombe glared at Tom. "You couldn't have stopped him?"

"I tried," Tom wailed. "I did. But you know what he's like."

The King's Warden regarded me. "Yes," he said finally. "I suppose I do."

He let me go. I really enjoyed breathing again. I even thought I might get out of this unscathed.

Then Lord Ashcombe smoothed out my collar where he'd crumpled it. That wasn't a good sign.

"Get on the horses," he said.

The King's Men had saddled the carriage horses they'd freed from the now-charred reins of our transport. The driver had taken one of them. Tom and Sally, with a final look of deep disappointment, climbed onto the horses beside him, one of the King's Men giving Sally a leg up.

"Sorry," I mumbled, and stepped toward the last mount.

Lord Ashcombe laid a finger on my chest. "Where do you think you're going?"

"You said to get on—"

Slowly, he shook his head.

Horror dawned as I realized what he meant. "But . . . we must be five, six miles from London!"

"You think so?" He stared off down the road, considering it. "I would have said seven."

"My lord . . . I . . . It was an *accident*."

Lord Ashcombe climbed into his saddle. "I understand. So if you'd rather not walk"—he jerked a thumb at the flaming heap behind me—"feel free to take the carriage."

CHAPTER

WELL, THERE'S ANOTHER THING TO REGRET.

On decent roads, it would have only taken a couple of hours to reach the city. But under the warming sun, the heavy snows of a violent winter had melted, leaving the roads nothing but long strips of muck. So it took nearly twice that time—and my poor, cramped, aching legs—to slog northward and catch sight of London Bridge.

I sighed. Originally, we'd planned to dismount on the south bank of the Thames and have a boat ferry us west to the Palace of Whitehall, where King Charles II waited for our return. But as I approached the bridge, I realized I'd forgotten something important.

I couldn't pay the boatman. When Tom, Sally, and I had left London in November, on a mission to spy for the king, Lord Ashcombe had given me a full coin purse to use as needed. It had come in awfully handy, first in Paris, and then while stranded on the coast of Devonshire. But since Lord Ashcombe had come to our rescue with the King's Men in December, he'd paid for everything we needed. I'd given the money back, leaving me broke.

Great. Now I'd have to walk all the way through the city, too. Still, tired as I was, there was one thing I welcomed.

Though I'd only been away four months, it felt like I'd been gone forever. All my life, I'd never left London: first, as a boy in the Cripplegate orphanage, and then, living with Master Benedict at the Blackthorn apothecary. My recent travels had been incredible—and terrifying—but as I crossed London Bridge, tired and muddy, I still felt an overwhelming relief.

Life had returned.

Last year, London had been under the grip of a terrible plague. When I'd left, the roads had been empty; nothing but fear and cries for the dead. Now the city was back.

Streets weren't packed like before the sickness, true. But there were people again: travelers, farmers leading sheep to market, carriage drivers screaming curses to get out of the road. It was jostling, deafening—and, in its way, beautiful.

Yet some darkness remained. Several of the stores I passed were damaged—windows smashed, doors cracked. In the wake of those who'd fled London came the desperate—or just plain criminal. Some houses had been looted.

My stomach churned to see it. I'd been away for so long. What about my shop? Had it been looted, too?

I was supposed to go straight to the palace. But I couldn't stop thinking about Blackthorn. My shop was north, not on the way to Whitehall. Yet I had to see it.

Legs aching, I quickened my pace.

I ran till I spotted the sign.

BLACKTHORN

it said, in big red letters. Underneath, in smaller printing,

RELIEFS FOR ALL MANNER OF MALIGNANT HUMORS

The words were surrounded by leaves of ivy, painted green, and a golden unicorn horn. The paint, once bright, was dull with neglect, the chains that held the sign dotted with rust. The windows were dirty, the doorstep covered with mud. It would take some care to bring it back to the way it should be.

But it was still here. No smashed glass, no splintered doorjamb. I nearly cried with relief. London might be my city, but this shop, this gift Master Benedict had given me, was my *home*.

And someone was waiting. A pigeon fluttered down from the flat-topped roof high above, flapping salt-and-pepper-speckled wings to land at my feet. She ran over my muddy boots, trilling a hello.

"Bridget!"

I picked her up. As we'd pulled onto the road this morning, I'd let her out of her cage to stretch her wings. She'd flown off into the blue, disappearing from sight almost immediately.

"Where have you been?" I complained. "I had to walk back here all alone."

She cooed and nestled into my hands. I suppose I couldn't blame her for being excited. Pigeons have an incredible sense of direction, and Bridget was keener than any bird I'd known. After we'd left Brighton with Lord Ashcombe three days ago, she'd grown increasingly restless. I think she'd understood we were going home.

At least she was all right. I cradled her in the crook of my arm and pulled out my key. I'd just clacked open the lock when I heard the call.

"Christopher?"

I turned. From the door of the Missing Finger, the tavern across the street, a tall girl of seventeen hurried across the road. It was Dorothy, the innkeeper's daughter, wearing her serving smock and apron. She hadn't bothered to put on a coat.

"It *is* you!" she said, and she hugged me, welcoming me home. If there was any doubt the plague was behind us, that put it to rest. The day I'd left, she wouldn't have touched me for all the wealth of kings.

She laughed and let me go. "What happened? You'd told me you'd be gone awhile; I didn't know you meant for months. I was worried the sickness— Are those *pistols*?"

Dorothy stared at my waist. Sure enough, two flintlocks hung from my belt, grips forward, in clear imitation of Lord Ashcombe. Though mine weren't nearly as nice as the King's Warden's. No fine walnut, no handles of pearl, no engraved barrel or trigger guard. Just simple, functional guns.

After our travels in Paris and Devonshire—and with

my enemy, the Raven, still at large—Lord Ashcombe had ordered me to start carrying a weapon. Tom wanted me to learn the sword, like him; he'd been training with one since we'd left for France. In the two months we'd spent stuck on the southern coast of England, held there by terrible storms and fear of the spreading plague, the King's Men had really taken Tom under their wing, coaching him in earnest. He'd not only practiced with his sword—an ancient holy blade called Eternity, given to him by the secret order of the Knights Templar in Paris—he'd learned techniques for spear, poleax, and halberd, too.

Tom was bigger and stronger than anyone I'd ever met, and he'd improved with startling speed. I'd already thought he was pretty good, considering how little training he'd had. Now there was no debate: He could use a sword, no mistake about it.

I wasn't such a natural. I'd taken some training with him—the sword, anyway; I didn't have the strength to handle halberds. But I'd gravitated to firearms instead. After an hour-long lecture from Lord Ashcombe about how gunpowder was not a toy—which I'd thought a bit much, and Tom and Sally not nearly enough—I'd practiced every day with musket, carbine, and pistol. I'd reached the point where

I could reliably shatter a bottle at twenty yards—forty with a musket—and, all in all, I was quite pleased with myself.

The King's Men saw how much I loved the smoke, the kick, and the boom the guns made. So a few days before we returned to London, before I let off my fireworks in celebration, they'd presented me with a pair of pistols. Ignoring Tom burying his face in his hands, and Sally's look of dread, I'd put them on proudly.

With Lord Ashcombe's permission, I'd kept them on my belt ever since. I'd also added gunpowder, wadding paper, and shot to my apothecary sash, which had once been Master Benedict's and which I now wore around my waist, under my clothes. So I had a dozen reloads, if it came to that.

It was no problem wearing the guns in the company of the King's Men. But here, back in London, Dorothy's surprise was well founded. As an apprentice, I wasn't allowed to carry weapons of any kind. I supposed I'd have to put them away. Just as I'd got used to the weight on my belt, too.

I couldn't tell Dorothy why I was really wearing them; I wasn't supposed to say I'd been working for the king. I'd told her instead I was going to stay with friends of my master's in Oxford, to avoid the plague. "Um . . . yes. Well . . . the roads are dangerous these days. So I figured . . . you know." I changed the subject. "Things look better here."

She brightened. "*So* much better. People are back. We even have lodgers again."

That was nice to hear. "Really?"

"Yes! A wool seller, and a farrier, and a new physician, too! Came a month ago, to help the city get back on its feet after the plague. My father's been trying to convince him to stay. With Dr. Parrett gone . . ."

Hearing that name filled me with sadness. Dr. Parrett had given his life for the people of this city—and, more directly, for me. He'd been a great man. I hoped the new physician would be even half as worthy.

"So," Dorothy said casually, "where's Tom?"

I smothered a grin. She'd had a thing for Tom for some time. Since we'd been away, he'd grown even taller, which was just ridiculous, and all the training and hard living had melted away any last bit of pudginess in him. With his hair long, he looked like a Viking. She'd lose her mind when she saw him.

"He's back, too," I said, keeping a straight face.

"Make sure he stops by to say hello."

"Oh, I will."

She left me with a friendly wave. I went inside.

And I was home.

The counter in the corner, worn and familiar. The display tables, laden with jars, beakers, and curios. The stuffed animal specimens, a favorite of Master Benedict's—and of mine.

But what struck me most was the smell. The heavy scent of spices, herbs, and flowers. It hit me like a wave, a rush of memories. It felt like my master, welcoming me back. Tears came hot and unwelcome.

Don't be sad, I heard him say. *I still live in your heart.*

And he did. I knew he watched over me, and that brought me such comfort. Yet at times like this, it never felt enough.

I wiped my eyes and walked around the shop. Bridget flapped from my arms and flew from table to table, saying hello to all the places she'd missed while we were away. I smiled as she found her favorite perch, high on the shelves among the jars. Now everything was just as I'd left it.

Almost.

The first thing that was different was the four-month layer of dust that covered everything. Master Benedict wouldn't have tolerated this at all. I'd need to give the place a thorough cleaning.

The second thing that was different was the letter.

Someone had placed a letter on the counter. It rested at an angle, propped against one of the antimony cups taken from the display table. They'd moved it onto the counter so I'd be sure to see it.

I picked up the letter, puzzled. On the front were two initials, written in simple calligraphy.

C. R.

C. R. Christopher Rowe. Me.

I flipped it over to see the back was sealed with wax. But there was no mark or crest pressed into the red splotch. Just a simple, featureless circle.

I frowned. Who'd left this here?

And how did they get in?

The front door had been locked. I checked the workshop; the door in the back was still barred, as I'd left it.

It occurred to me that I'd been in a rush last November, when we'd hurried off to France. Had I missed the letter then?

No. There was an empty ring in the dust on the table, from where the antimony cup had been taken. Whoever had left this must have done so recently.

I made to break the seal on the back, but I didn't get the chance. From behind me, the bell rang overhead as the front door opened.

I assumed it was Dorothy again. "Hey, did you—" I began.

And then I stopped, staring in shocked delight at the man who'd entered my shop.

"Simon!"

It was Simon Chastellain, the dashing young vicomte d'Aviron. He was the nephew of Marin Chastellain, Master Benedict's oldest friend. I'd met them for the first time in Paris.

I couldn't believe Simon was here. "What are you doing in London?" I said. "And how did you know I was back?"

He didn't answer. He stepped toward me, arms forward, an odd look on his face. I stuffed the mysterious letter I was holding into my coat, thinking he was coming to give me a hug.

Instead, he collapsed in my arms.

His sudden weight made me stagger. I bumped into the counter, heard the antimony cup fall over and roll off, dinging dully across the floorboards.

I tried to hold him. "Simon? What . . . ?"

My hands, my arms wrapped around him, felt warm and wet. As he slipped downward, I saw why. My hands were covered in blood.

And there was a dagger in Simon's back.

CHAPTER

MY VOICE CAME OUT A CROAK.

"Help," I said.

Then louder. "Help! *Help!*"

Simon slid to the floor, conscious but confused. "Christopher?"

He tried to roll over. I stopped him. The dagger, stuck between his ribs, was twisted at an odd angle. If he put his weight on it, it would drive the blade deep into his lungs.

I laid him on his stomach, pressed him to the floor. "Stay there," I said. "Don't move. *Someone help!*"

Simon looked to be in shock. He reached behind him,

groping for whatever was causing him pain. I kept his hand away.

"Don't *move*," I said, and I shoved his arms under his body. It was an ugly thing, that blade, sticking through his coat, but I left it where it was. My master had taught me that.

If something pierces the body, he'd said, *show great care before removing it. The object may be the only thing preventing catastrophic bleeding.*

What do I do? I asked him.

Find a surgeon. Immediately.

I didn't know about a surgeon. One had lived a couple of streets away, but he'd left last summer with the plague. I had no idea if he'd returned, or if he was even alive.

But—Dorothy. She'd mentioned a physician.

I didn't like leaving Simon, but I didn't have a choice. I pressed his arms in again, tucking them under his stomach. "Stay that way, all right? I'll be back."

Simon still sounded confused, but he nodded. "What happened?"

I didn't answer. Instead, I ran across the road, shouting, "Help!"

Dorothy met me at the door to the Missing Finger. "Christopher? What's wrong?"

"My friend—he's been injured. Is that physician here? I need him."

"Yes, he's in . . . Your friend? Is it Tom?"

"What? No, not Tom. *Where's the physician?*"

He was in the dining room. The man was stocky, not overly tall, with a broad mustache. He sat across from a curly-haired boy dressed in the blue apron of an apprentice. The man looked up, as did the few other patrons, who stopped drinking to watch the commotion.

"What's the trouble?" he said, in a heavy northern accent.

I didn't want a gaggle of onlookers. A stabbing was sure to bring them. So I just said, "Simon . . . my friend . . . he's had an accident."

The doctor had already begun to rise. He'd seen my bloody hands. "Get my bag," he commanded his apprentice.

The boy ran upstairs as the two of us returned to Blackthorn. The doctor paused in the doorway when he saw Simon on the floor, the dagger sticking out of him.

He glanced over at me. "Some accident."

"It wasn't . . ." I didn't have time to explain. I didn't even know what was happening. "He came in like this."

The doctor gave me a speculative look, but only briefly. "We have to get him up. Where's your bed?"

"Upstairs."

We each took one arm. Simon screamed as we lifted him. I looked over at the doctor.

He shook his head. "Can't be helped."

We went slowly, careful not to bump Simon into the wall. "You didn't take the dagger out," the doctor noted as we inched our way up the narrow stairs.

"My master said not to."

"Good lad."

The doctor's apprentice arrived, clutching the doctor's satchel, as his master and I carried Simon into my bedroom. The place was a mess of books. Piles upon piles of them, stacked so high they teetered like trees bending in the wind.

The doctor made us a path by kicking them out of the way. The books toppled, knocking down others in a rumble of leather and paper. I winced to see them treated so badly.

The doctor's only care was his patient. Gently, we laid Simon on the bed, facedown. He cried out, then lay still, breathing in short, ragged gasps.

"Move aside." The doctor bumped me backward. The apprentice stepped more lightly, weaving between the books to my desk. He cleared a space on top, then began drawing out his master's tools.

I was surprised to see so many saws and blades. "Are you a surgeon?"

"I was in the army," the doctor said, as if that answered the question. Which I supposed it did. He'd have seen much worse than this. "I'm not part of the guild, if that's what you're asking. You planning on letting them know?"

It was a serious question. By law, the Company of Barbers and Surgeons performed all operations. He'd be in big trouble for doing this. "No."

"Then go on, get your master. I'm going to need some things."

"I don't have a master," I said.

He frowned. "You're talking nonsense, boy. Isn't that your master's shop downstairs?"

"No, it's mine. It's . . . My master was murdered. Last year. He left me the shop, and this home. I was supposed to get a new master, but the Apothecaries' Guild's been ignoring me."

The physician snorted. "Politics, is it?"

I nodded.

"Well, then," he said, "let's annoy the guilds together, shall we?" And he grinned. "I need water, at least four buckets of it, and as much cloth as you can spare. When that's done, bring me whatever you use to cover wounds."

"What about something for the pain?" I said.

"Not until I'm finished. Go on now. And you"—he nodded to his apprentice—"get these blasted books out of my way."

I did as the physician asked, stamping down the panic in my chest. Cloth was no problem; we kept tons of rags for cleaning spills. As for water, normally I'd have a barrel full, but what was in the store was four months old and stagnant. I'd need to go to the well.

How I wished Tom and Sally were here. I spotted Dorothy hovering by the door to the Missing Finger, worried. So I enlisted her help instead. We each grabbed a pair of buckets, filled them, and brought them up the stairs, puffing.

The apprentice took them from us at the bedroom door. The doctor's stocky frame blocked our view, but I could see he'd cut away Simon's clothes.

There was blood on the sheets. Dorothy blanched at the sight of it. She grew even whiter at Simon's howls as the doctor began to work. I led her back down to the shop.

Bridget flew to me from her perch, alarmed by the

commotion. I held her just a moment, then put her aside. "I need to send a message to Whitehall."

What I'd said was so unexpected, Dorothy stopped thinking about the horror upstairs and stared. "The *palace*?"

"Yes." I scribbled a note on some paper I pulled from under the counter. "Can you find someone to take this to Lord Ashcombe? Make sure it goes straight to him, and that he reads it immediately. I'll pay for the courier, just come find me for the penny."

"*Ashcombe?* The *King's Warden*? Christopher . . . what have you got yourself into?"

"Please, Dorothy. I really need your help."

She stared at me for a moment, then glanced at the pistols on my belt. She grabbed the letter. "I'll take it myself."

"Thank you," I said, grateful.

She stopped, regarding me from the door. "You've changed," she said.

Had I? Then how come I still felt like the useless, clueless boy stuck in the middle of things he didn't understand? I couldn't even keep my friends safe.

Dorothy left. I shut out Simon's cries and got to work.

CHAPTER

MY FIRST TASK WAS TO MAKE THE

honey balm. That was Master Benedict's recipe to spread over wounds. Once that was done, I took the jar upstairs, leaving it in the corridor outside my bedroom. I then returned to the workshop to make some pain reliever. Willow bark extract would do nothing for this level of hurt; I'd need to boil a poppy infusion.

Bridget fluttered about the workshop, agitated by Simon's howling, but I had no more time to calm her. Again I wished Tom and Sally were here. Fortunately, working distracted me, and Simon's cries faded as the minutes passed. I hoped that was because the surgery was ending, and not because . . .

I shuddered. I didn't even want to imagine it.

When the poppy was ready, I carried it up. Just in time, it seemed, because the doctor and his apprentice were already wrapping Simon with bandages. They'd dipped into the honey balm; I could see it smeared all over Simon's back.

"Leave the pot there," the doctor ordered. I did as he asked, then went back downstairs to pace the shop and wait.

When Lord Ashcombe arrived, he was flanked by four of the King's Men. Two stayed with the horses, while the others accompanied him inside.

"Where's Chastellain?" he said.

"Upstairs," I said. "The doctor—"

Before I could finish, the doctor came down. He stopped short, hands bundled in a rag, clothes stained with blood.

He stared at the King's Men, at their leather tabards emblazoned with the king's coat of arms. Then he spotted Lord Ashcombe—and turned to me, stunned.

He'd recognized the King's Warden. With the man's distinctive black style, scar, eye patch, and injured hand, it was hard not to. I made introductions anyway.

"Lord Richard Ashcombe, Marquess of Chillingham," I said. "And Doctor . . ." It finally occurred to me that I'd never heard the man's name.

"Kemp," the doctor said, with a slight bow of the head. "John Kemp, of Newcastle."

That explained the northern accent. He gave me a small, bemused smile. I could imagine what he was thinking. *A masterless, pistol-wielding apprentice, and the king's right-hand man. What have I stumbled into?* I'm glad he didn't ask.

"What news?" Lord Ashcombe said.

"Good, I think," Dr. Kemp said, and I breathed a sigh of relief. "Your friend has an excellent chance of recovery."

"I thought he had a dagger in his back."

"Aha. Yes. Normally does little to improve a man's lifespan. But in this case, I'd say he has the luck of the angels."

The doctor finished wiping something in the rag, then held it out for us to see.

It was the dagger. Lord Ashcombe took it, turned it over.

The weapon was an odd shape I'd never seen before. It had a large conical pommel and a smooth cylindrical grip. There wasn't much of a hilt; the grip simply rounded up to where it held the steel. As for the blade itself, it was long and flat—though the point was badly bent.

I stared at it. "*This* didn't kill him?"

"Like I said, luck of the angels. When our would-be

murderer stabbed— What was your friend's name again? Simon? Simon's spine got in the way."

The doctor took the dagger back to demonstrate. "The tip of the blade bent when it hit the vertebra, and so couldn't penetrate farther. It slipped sideways instead— stuck in him at an angle, you see? It never got through to the innards."

Lord Ashcombe studied the dagger as Dr. Kemp continued. "There's damage to the muscle, of course, and he'll be in quite a bit of pain for a few weeks, but as long as we stave off infection, he should recover. And thank his heavenly guardian. An inch up or down, he'd be paralyzed. Right or left, he'd be dead."

Lord Ashcombe nodded, then turned to me. "Who did this?"

"I don't know," I said. "Simon just came in and collapsed."

"Did you check for witnesses?"

I flushed. "I didn't think to . . . I was worried about . . . No."

Lord Ashcombe commanded the King's Men to search outside. Then he asked the doctor, "Can we speak to him?"

"You can try, but you won't get much of anything out of him today. I administered a heavy dose of our young friend's poppy, so he'll be addled beyond reason. If not already asleep."

Lord Ashcombe clomped upstairs, mud tracking from his boots. I followed, behind the physician. The apprentice was doing what he could to clean up after Dr. Kemp. Though I'd never get the blood out of those sheets.

Simon dozed on his stomach, mouth open, drooling, a heavy bandage wrapped around his chest. Crimson spotted the cloth on his back.

"Chastellain," Lord Ashcombe said. "Vicomte."

Simon moaned faintly.

"Did you see who attacked you?"

"Mn?"

"Your attacker. Did you see him?"

"No. Back. Something . . . hurt."

"Who might have done this?"

I could think of someone. Someone very likely indeed. "Was it the Raven?" I said. I knelt beside the bed. "Simon? Was it the Raven?"

"Hm? . . . No."

"You didn't see who attacked you," Lord Ashcombe said. "How do you know it wasn't?"

"Because," Simon mumbled, drifting off. "The Raven is dead."

CHAPTER

I STARED AT SIMON.

The Raven—the man who'd murdered Marin Chastellain, Simon's uncle, Master Benedict's lifelong friend—the man who'd promised to murder me—was dead?

I couldn't believe it. "How?" I shook Simon's shoulder. "How do you know the Raven's dead? Simon!"

"Here, now." Dr. Kemp hauled me up by the crook of my arm. "You know better than that."

"Yes. Of course. Sorry." The poppy had left Simon in no state to speak. And anyway, he really needed to rest. Master Benedict would have been embarrassed by what I'd done, and that made me ashamed.

"Sorry," I said again, as much to my master as anyone else. I just felt so confused. All these months, the shadow of the Raven had loomed over me. How could he just be dead?

"We're expected at the palace," Lord Ashcombe said, "and we won't get any answers here today. Let's go."

I didn't like leaving Simon behind, but there really was nothing else that we could do. I nodded, my mind a whirl. I was so out of it, I almost forgot the good doctor's fee.

"I have a few coins here somewhere," I said. Actually, I had a lot of them, but they were tucked into the mattress Simon was on, and I didn't think it prudent to go digging for gold in front of strangers. "I'll bring them to the Missing Finger."

Lord Ashcombe overruled me. "Send a bill to Whitehall."

Dr. Kemp raised his eyebrows, again giving me that bemused smile. I didn't explain. I did, however, finally remember I hadn't given him my name. "I'm Christopher Rowe."

"Very well, Mr. Rowe," he said, still smiling. "With your permission, I'll return to care for our patient as needed."

Lord Ashcombe checked with the King's Men; they hadn't been able to find any witnesses to the attack. Leaving one of the soldiers behind to stand guard in case the assassin came back to finish the job, Lord Ashcombe ordered me to take the man's horse. I collected Bridget, then mounted.

The warhorse made me a little nervous. Tom, Sally, and I had been taught to ride while waiting to return to London, but I'd always practiced on the carriage horses, which were smaller and of calmer temperament. This beast's power was kind of frightening.

"Problem?" Lord Ashcombe said.

I didn't want to admit being scared. Instead, I said, "Thank you for coming to help. I just . . . I can't believe the Raven's dead."

"Why not?"

"Well . . . I mean . . . he was so good at manipulating things. I thought he'd be too clever to get caught."

"Every blackguard thinks he's invincible," Lord Ashcombe said. "Let that dagger in Simon's back be a reminder. Peasant or noble, we all go out the same."

I'd never been to Whitehall. The palace, home of English kings since Henry VIII, was to the west of London, round the bend of the Thames, well outside the city walls. Tom and I had set out a few times to go see it on one of our rare holidays, but it was miles from where we lived, and we'd always got distracted along the way.

Now, as I rode in with Lord Ashcombe, I saw it lived up to its reputation. The palace was a sprawling labyrinth, every part built in a different style, from the simple brick-and-stone of Scotland Yard, to the sloping roofs and gray clock tower of the Horse Guards barracks, to the Holbein Gate, which looked like a miniature keep with octagonal towers at each corner. It loomed above the main through-way, its twelve-foot-high arch wide enough to allow oversize wagons into the city.

Behind the buildings to the east were the docks on the Thames; to the west stretched the vast green expanse of Saint James's Park. If we'd continued south, we'd have seen the grand gallery overlooking the Privy Garden, complete with marble statues and an apple orchard, and Westminster Gate beyond, following the road southwest, away from London.

At the moment, however, all traffic was stalled. The Holbein Gate was closed, causing a jam of carriages, carts, and pedestrians, all grumbling at the holdup.

From the frown on Lord Ashcombe's face, this wasn't normal. One of the King's Men took the lead, carving a path through the crowd with his horse, crying, "Make way!

Make way for the Marquess of Chillingham!" The rest of us followed in his wake.

The gate that led into the palace itself was off to the left. A smaller line waited here, at a semicircle of posts rising from the mud in the road. Four guards stood watch at the entrance. A fifth soldier was arguing with a pair of finely dressed men at the front of the queue.

The shorter of the pair was red-faced, near shouting. His companion, a man with a trimmed beard and gold spectacles, waited quietly, hand on his chin.

"Another English slight," the short man said in a thick Scottish accent. "We have every right to enter. Let us pass!"

Lord Ashcombe ignored the argument. He dismounted and spoke to the guards near the entryway. "What's going on?"

"Don't know, General," the sergeant at arms said. "We were told to seal off the palace. No one in or out."

"Ordered by whom?"

"The captain. Think the order came from the chamberlain, though."

Lord Ashcombe didn't like what he was hearing. Fortunately, the rules didn't apply to him. "With me," he said. I followed him inside, sticking as close as I could, Bridget tucked in the crook of my arm.

The Scotsman at the gate was outraged. "Why does *he* get to go in—Ashcombe! *Ashcombe!* Don't pretend you can't hear me!"

I looked up at Lord Ashcombe as we strode into the court.

"I'm not pretending," he said. "I just don't care."

Lord Ashcombe appeared to know where we were going, which was good, because with the way the palace corridors twisted and turned, I was completely lost.

"Remove your pistols," he said.

"My lord?"

"Only guards enter the king's presence armed."

Right. I unbuckled my belt. "What do I do with them?"

"An attendant will take them. The bird, too."

We finally reached our destination: a somewhat over-decorated antechamber, walls plastered with portraits, the tables layered with Oriental rugs. I was relieved to see Tom and Sally were already there. They'd changed out of their traveling clothes and now looked rather fine: Tom in a sharp blue doublet, black breeches, and hose, and Sally in a red-dish gown that matched her auburn hair rather prettily.

As for me, I suddenly felt self-conscious. Still dirty from

the road, I smelled of mud, smoke, and horse. And was that Simon's blood on my breeches?

Behind the others were a pair of guards, both with halberds, and another pair near the door. Three servants hovered against the wall; one of them stepped forward to relieve me of my pistols, and, with a slight look of distaste, my pigeon as well. I felt a pang of regret as the man hurried from the room. I'd get Bridget back, of course. I wasn't so sure about the guns.

A second servant brushed as much of the dirt off me as he could, clucking his tongue in disapproval. He positioned me next to Tom, who looked nervous, sweating.

"What took you so long?" he whispered, voice cracking.

I hardly knew where to begin. But I didn't want to say anything in front of all these strangers. "Why is the palace locked down?" I whispered back.

Sally spread her hands. "We don't know. But soldiers are everywhere."

Then there was no time left to say anything. The guards slammed the butts of their halberds against the floor and opened the door.

And the king entered the room.

CHAPTER

WE'D MET CHARLES II BEFORE— twice, actually—but I still felt the thrill of meeting our sovereign. Sally smoothed her gown nervously, then clasped her hands to keep them still. Tom, who loved His Majesty the most, stared straight ahead, trembling and sweating. I shrank a little, embarrassed by my ragtag appearance.

Charles, flanked by four of the King's Men and a pair of servants, cut an imposing figure. Except for Tom, he was much taller than anyone else here, around six-foot-two, with a curly wig that fell past his shoulders. He wasn't the most attractive fellow: long face and heavy brow with a dark complexion and sagging cheeks. But he carried himself with extraordinary grace, and his smile, always ready, made you feel like you were the most important person in the room.

He smiled at the three of us now, striding our way. "My friends," he said warmly. "My dear, dear friends." And he offered me his hand.

I was almost too startled to take it. Bending down on one knee, "Your Majesty" was all I could mumble.

He gripped my shoulders as I stood. "Christopher. How worried I was for you all when I heard the news of your shipwreck. How I prayed for your safe return."

Tom's eyes bulged. "*You* . . . prayed for *us*?" he said. He was so stunned, he forgot to say "Your Majesty."

"Every night," Charles said seriously, and he offered Tom his hand next.

Tom kneeled, positively glowing. But being a couple of inches taller than the king had its drawbacks. Charles was wearing a feathered, wide-brimmed, silver-trimmed hat. As Tom rose, his forehead bumped the hat's brim and knocked it from the king's head.

Tom was mortified. "Sorry, Your Majesty," he said as he scrambled to retrieve it.

Charles just laughed. "Odd's fish, how can you be so

tall? No, you keep it." The king placed his hat on Tom's head. "A gift."

Tom's embarrassment turned to awe. He looked at me with the widest grin.

Then the king moved on to Sally, who curtsied. "Such loveliness returned to Court," he said. She blushed furiously.

More serious, he said, "And your hand. Is it better?"

Sally had nearly been killed in Paris. As it was, a head injury had rendered her left hand almost immobile. Then, in Devonshire, she'd injured it further when she got run through with a knife. She seemed surprised the king even knew about it.

"Uh . . . yes, Your Majesty. It's improving."

"Excellent." He patted her hand. "On to business. First—Christopher."

"Y-yes, sire?" I stammered.

"I can never repay the service you have done me, nor compensate you adequately for the dangers you have braved. Nevertheless, I must insist you not set fire to any more of my things."

My face grew hot. "Sorry."

I'd been trying not to think about what punishment he'd dole out for what I'd done. But he apparently considered the matter settled, because he moved on. "Very well. I have gifts for the three of you. I had hoped to give them today, but something else must occupy my time."

He glanced at Lord Ashcombe, whose gaze suddenly sharpened. I guessed he was talking about why the palace was locked down, but he didn't say anything more about it.

"Regardless," the king continued, "I have one gift with me, so I may as well offer it. Sally?"

He smiled as one of his servants placed a proclamation in his hand, which he read. "'I declare that on this, the day of our Lord, the third of March, 1666, I do accept the care and guardianship of Sara-Claire Adeline Marie Deschamps, of London, late of the Cripplegate orphanage, to be established according to the laws, and so on. Signed, Charles R., King of England,' et cetera."

It took a moment for us to understand what had just happened. When we did, Sally nearly burst into tears. She covered her mouth with her hands, eyes shining.

The king had taken her as his ward.

That meant, from now on, the Crown would be responsible for looking after her. She'd have someplace to live, and food on her table, and clothes as she needed, until she got married.

I couldn't believe it. Sally had been terrified about what would happen to her once we returned to London. Before we'd left, she'd been employed as a servant to one of the court ladies. With her hand injured, it was unlikely anyone would take her back.

While in Brighton, I'd asked Lord Ashcombe privately if he'd see that she be looked after. I'd only meant that he might inquire if anyone at Court would consider hiring her again. I hadn't imagined *this*.

"Are you pleased, my dear?" Charles said.

She stood there, hands covering her face, and sobbed.

He laughed. "Excellent. Until tomorrow, then. Richard?"

Lord Ashcombe followed him out of the room.

CHAPTER

WE DIDN'T GET ANY TIME TO CELE-
brate. Tom and I had barely crowded around Sally to congratulate her when a pair of servants stepped in.

Tom and I were to be given a room at the palace. Sally
was told, with many apologies, that they had been unable
to find empty quarters suitable for her at Whitehall, so she'd
be housed at Berkshire House instead, which was all the
way on the other side of Saint James's Park.

I was disappointed by that. I knew from my time in
Paris that space in any palace was hard to come by. Nobles,
courtiers, and other hangers-on measured their importance
by how close they lived to the king. The lower rungs

considered themselves lucky to receive even a closet turned into a makeshift bedroom, with nothing but a palliasse and a lantern to fight the dark.

Still, I liked Sally being around. I liked how cheerful she was, even when things weren't going well. I liked how sometimes she'd sing, under her breath, not even realizing she was doing it. And I liked . . . well, I liked a lot of things, I guess.

It wasn't as if she was gone forever, I knew. Nonetheless, I was disappointed—and maybe a bit worried. Because when the servants escorted her away, the guards went with her. It didn't feel quite natural. Almost like they were protecting her.

Was I reading too much into it? Maybe. I still didn't think it was anything good.

As for Tom and me, our quarters ended up much better than a closet. The room had clearly once been a parlor; the couches and tables that had occupied the space were still there, piled in one corner. In their place were two small beds opposite the window, which had an amazing view of the Thames. A log burned in the fireplace, filling the room with a smoky warmth.

In one corner was a bucket of water. I asked the servant who'd escorted us if this was meant for washing, and was told with barely restrained amusement that all the rooms in the palace had them. Apparently, Whitehall had a bit of a history of the buildings catching fire. If one broke out, we were to grab our bucket and rush to the blaze. I avoided Tom's eyes as this was said.

At least I got my pistols back. They were waiting for me on my bed, as was Bridget. She flapped about, from the furniture to the window, restless, while Tom admired his new hat in the window's reflection.

"What do you think you'll get as a gift?" he said.

"I don't know," I said. "But we'll both get one, I'm sure."

"What do you mean? I already have mine."

"The king made Sally his ward. I'm pretty sure he's planned more for you than a hat."

"But it's so splendid. Don't you think?"

To tell the truth, I thought it was a bit flamboyant for Tom, with the feathers and all. But he was so proud, I wouldn't say a word against it. "Makes you look like a musketeer."

"Really? They're incredible soldiers, you know."

Tom was clearly in a great mood if he was saying nice things about the French. He admired his hat a bit more, then asked, "Why were you gone so long, anyway? It shouldn't have taken you *that* much time to walk here."

I sat up, surprised. I'd all but forgotten what had happened just a couple of hours ago. Meeting the king does something to the brain, I guess.

"Simon's here," I said. "Someone tried to kill him."

"What?"

I told Tom everything that had happened. He listened, horrified, and when I was finished, he had the exact same question I had. "Was it the Raven?"

Bridget flapped from the window and landed on my shoulder, poking her beak into my hair. I took her in my hands and held her.

"According to Simon," I said, "the Raven's dead."

"*Dead?* How? That's incredible!"

"I suppose."

"You *suppose?*"

"I don't know. Something doesn't feel right. How can the Raven be dead?"

"He's just a man, Christopher."

"Lord Ashcombe said the same thing."

"There you go, then." Tom flopped onto his bed. "So you didn't see who attacked Simon?"

"It happened outside. I was in the shop. . . ."

I trailed off.

"What is it?" Tom said.

"The letter."

"What letter?"

I'd tossed my coat on my bed when I came in. Now I put Bridget down and fished the letter from the inside pocket.

"This," I said, holding it up. The attack on Simon had made me forget all about it. "It was waiting for me on the counter, at Blackthorn. You didn't go by the shop, did you?"

Tom shook his head. "We came straight to Whitehall."

"So who put it there?" I said.

"Does it say who it's from?"

"I don't recognize the handwriting."

"I meant *in* the letter."

"I haven't read it yet."

Tom raised his eyebrows. "Then . . . maybe you should?"

Good point.

Why *hadn't* I read it?

Because, Master Benedict said, *in the back of your mind, you think it's from the Raven.*

The Raven's dead, I replied.

Wasn't he?

Tom was looking at me strangely. This was stupid. Just open the thing.

With a deep breath, I cracked the wax seal. Then, with growing amazement, I read the message inside.

CHAPTER

"WHAT IS IT?" TOM SAID NERVOUSLY.

"I . . . don't know."

I showed him the letter.

> *An oath was made, a promise sworn,*
> *To those who wished to bind him.*
>
> *But he returned, and offered scorn,*
> *And so they come to find him.*
>
> *You will know the key when you see*
> *the truth. Remember Paris.*

Tom looked at me, worried. "What does this mean?"

I had no idea. I read the whole thing again, mind racing.

And so they come to find him, it said. Find whom?

Me?

I'd returned. And someone *had* said they'd come for me. The Raven. Dead or not.

But as I read the letter over, I couldn't make the rest of the rhyme match. Had I sworn an oath to anyone? And then "offered scorn," whatever that was supposed to mean?

I couldn't recall anything like that. So far, I'd kept every promise I'd made.

So if the riddle wasn't meant for me . . . then for whom?

"Simon, maybe?" Tom said.

Someone *had* attacked him. But I wasn't sure he fit the "returned" part. "I don't think Simon's ever been to London," I said.

Tom thought about it. "What about the king? Charles returned to the throne, almost six years ago. And he gets threatened a *lot.*"

That was a definite possibility. I mulled it over.

You're missing something in the message, Master Benedict said.

He was right; once again, my brain was a jumble. I'd got so hung up on the riddle, I'd forgotten the even more curious part.

"We should solve the cipher," I said. "There might be more of a clue in there."

"Do you know how?"

"Well . . . the line above the code says we need a key. And that we should remember Paris. So . . ."

"Use the Vigenère's square cipher!" Tom said.

"You remembered," I said. "I'm impressed."

"It's the hat. Makes me smarter."

That made me laugh. "All right, monsieur. What's the key that'll solve the code?"

"Er . . ."

This was always the tricky part. "Let's write out the square to start."

I had a quill and ink in my sash, but there was no paper in our room, other than the letter itself, which I didn't want to write on. So, taking Bridget with us, we went to find some.

And quickly got lost.

All the corridors looked the same to me, with their paintings and curios and carpets. Twice we were shuffled out of what was clearly someone's private chambers, the second time by a lady shouting, "Out! How dare you! Ruffians!"

"This place is a maze," Tom said, flustered. Fortunately, a passing servant, an elderly gentleman with a dignified bearing and ponderous speech, took pity on us.

"May I be of assistance, sirs?"

"Could you send some paper to our room, please? And . . . um . . ." I looked up and down the hall. "Could you maybe also tell us where our room is?"

"Certainly, sir." The man, whose name was Dobson, already seemed to know where we'd been housed, which impressed me. Keeping track of the ever-changing guests living in the palace couldn't be easy.

"I don't suppose you have a map," I joked, after he'd led us back.

"Of course, sir. Would you like a copy?"

I blinked. "Really?"

"His Majesty had a floor plan commissioned. Helps sort things out, you see. I'll bring it at once."

We waited, me thinking about ciphers and Tom admiring his hat, until the man returned. He handed us

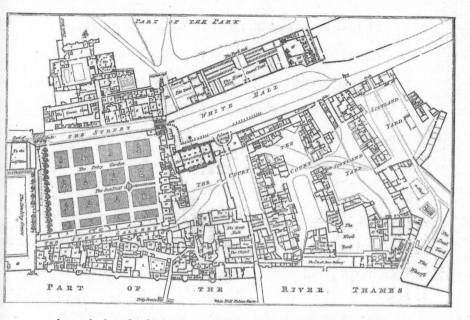

a broad sheaf of blank paper and, as promised, a map of the palace.

"It only shows the ground floor, sir," Dobson said, "but perhaps it will be of use."

"What do all these numbers mean?" Tom asked.

"An indication of who is lodged where."

He used my quill to mark our quarters for us. We were on the east side, beside the Thames, in a little room numbered *40*. "Who's that?" I asked.

"Sir William Killigrew," Dobson said. "The Queen's Vice-Chamberlain and member of Parliament for Richmond in Yorkshire. Bit of a playwright as well, I understand."

"I'll have to thank him for allowing us to use his parlor."

"Hm . . . perhaps not."

In other words, Sir William Killigrew was furious that we'd taken some of his space. "I see . . . In that case, we'll avoid him at all costs."

Dobson nodded sagely. "Wisdom is a blessing, sir."

I needed a desk. Tom and I pulled a table from the pile of furniture in our room and righted it. Bridget marched in front of the window as I wrote out Vigenère's square.

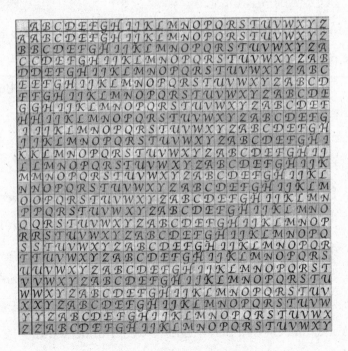

"Now we need to figure out what the key is," I said. "The message says it's about the truth of what happened in Paris. So what is that?"

"Finding the Templars?" Tom suggested.

As good a place as any to start. I wrote out the cipher, then repeated the key above it.

T E M P L A R S T E M P L A R S T E
M O I U R H J B X A M G X B H B L L

"I don't remember how the rest of this works," Tom said.

"To decipher something," I reminded him, "we start on the row with the first letter of the key: *T.* Then we search to the right, until we find the letter of the code: *M.* Then we go up to the top of the column . . . and that should be the first letter of the message."

"*T,*" Tom said.

"Yes. And we write that down."

T E M P L A R S T E M P L A R S T E
M O I U R H J B X A M G X B H B L L
T

"Now we just keep doing that for each letter. Next in the key is *E* . . . go across to find the *O* . . . and up to get . . ."

"*K*," Tom said.

T E M P L A R S T E M P L A R S T E
M O I U R H J B X A M G X B H B L L
T K

"Next, start with *M*, go to *I*, and we get . . . *W*."

T E M P L A R S T E M P L A R S T E
M O I U R H J B X A M G X B H B L L
T K W

I already didn't like what we were seeing. And I was right not to. Deciphering the whole message left us with nonsense.

T E M P L A R S T E M P L A R S T E
M O I U R H J B X A M G X B H B L L
T K W F G H S J E W A R M B Q J S H

"It didn't work," Tom said.

I shook my head. *TEMPLARS* wasn't the key.

Tom thought some more. "What about 'treasure'?"

We tried that next.

T R E A S U R E T R E A S U R E T R
M O I U R H J B X A M G X B H B L L
T X E U Z N S X E J I G F H Q X S U

It didn't get us anywhere, either.

I sighed. Figuring out a key was never easy. We'd just have to keep going until we found it. Tom and I tried whatever we could think of that fit the riddle. *ASSASSIN. LOUISXIV. KING.* Even *RAVEN.*

I really hoped that last one wouldn't be the answer— and it wasn't. All I ended up with was a similar jumble of letters that meant nothing.

"Maybe we've got the wrong idea," Tom said.

"How do you mean?"

"What if it's a different code?"

That was a possibility. If the cipher wasn't Vigenère, then the square would never give us the answer. But it was just as possible we hadn't figured out the right key yet. After all, the only cipher we'd used in Paris that needed a key was Vigenère— Wait.

Maybe *that's* what the hint about Paris meant. We were supposed to use the same key we'd used to solve the riddle there.

The key in Paris turned out to be *RAI.* Excited, I tried it.

R A I R A I R A I R A I R A I R A I R A I

M O I U R H J B X A M G X B H B L L

V O A D R Z S B P J M Y G B Z K L D

But that didn't work, either.

Now I was totally stumped. Further thoughts were interrupted by a knock on the door.

Dobson had returned. "The Marquess of Chillingham requests your company, sirs. At your earliest convenience."

Diplomatic, our Dobson. What Lord Ashcombe had likely said was *Get those two idiots here now.*

"What did you do?" Tom said to me as Dobson led us through the palace.

"Nothing," I said. "Why do you always assume everything's my fault?"

He shrugged. "I find it saves time."

As it turned out, neither of us was in trouble. Lord Ashcombe received us in an office; I wasn't sure if it was his. Not that it mattered. I'd left the map of Whitehall on the desk, so I had no idea how I'd find this room again.

Lord Ashcombe was staring out the window, looking down at the Privy Garden. The marble statues were lit by torches, glowing against the darkness of the night. The King's Warden held something. With his back turned, I couldn't tell what it was.

"Lockdown's over," he said.

"What caused it, my lord?"

"Murder. Servant girl of seventeen, by the name of Mary Brickenham."

Tom covered his mouth in horror.

"When did this happen?" I said.

"She brought lunch to the Countess of Castlemaine at one thirty, so sometime later than that. Her body was found in the charcoal house. Just lying there, atop a pile toward the back."

I frowned. Given the cold weather, servants would be in and out of the charcoal house all day. It would have been trivially easy for the killer to shovel charcoal over the body, hide it in one of the piles. Mary wouldn't have been found for days.

So either someone didn't want to give themselves away by getting charcoal all over their clothes, or . . . "The killer wanted her discovered."

Lord Ashcombe nodded. "This murder wasn't random. There's a message in it."

"To whom?" Tom said. "Saying what?"

"I don't know."

"Then why do you think it's a message?" I said.

"The weapon was left in the body. She'd been stabbed through the heart, from the back. With this."

He slid the item he held across the desk. It was a dagger. Flat pommel, unadorned grip, narrow hilt, long blade.

I stared at it. "That's the kind of dagger Simon was stabbed with."

"Exactly." Lord Ashcombe regarded me. "Whoever killed Mary Brickenham wanted Chastellain dead just the same."

CHAPTER

LORD ASHCOMBE HAD NO ANSWER
as to why anyone would want a servant and a French
vicomte dead. According to him, Mary Brickenham was
well liked and a decent worker, with no suitors or romantic
involvements. He'd also been able to discover that Simon
had visited Whitehall earlier that day, looking for me.

I regretted being stuck in the palace. Dr. Kemp had promised us Simon would be all right after his surgery, but I still
would have liked to check on him. Lord Ashcombe said he'd
ask Simon tomorrow if he'd seen Mary while he was here. In
the meantime, Lord Ashcombe pointed out both daggers had a
symbol on them, pressed into the steel near the hilt.

It was a *W*, imprinted inside a circle. It reminded me of the witches' marks we'd seen in Devonshire.

"It's not that," Lord Ashcombe said when I mentioned it. "It's a maker's mark, hammered by the blacksmith. We're trying to identify which man made them. And then, from there, who bought them."

"Any leads, my lord?"

"All we know so far is this mark isn't from any blacksmith in London. We'll have to check with other cities."

That would take weeks. Far too long to be helpful, I thought. But Lord Ashcombe pointed out that the mark told us something, regardless. If the killer—or killers, no reason to assume there was only one—got their weapons outside the city, they very likely came from somewhere else, as well.

When he was finished with the daggers, I showed him the letter I'd found in my house.

He frowned as he read it. "No idea who it's from?"

I shook my head. "Tom and I have been trying to decipher the code at the bottom. That might give us a clue. But we haven't been able to figure it out."

Lord Ashcombe looked pensive. "Someone may be able to help with that."

"Who, my lord?"

"You'll meet him tomorrow. For now, get some sleep. The king rises early, and he wants to speak with you in the morning."

Sleep well before a private meeting with the king? Not likely. I spent the night dreaming of angry, black-feathered birds.

THURSDAY, MARCH 4, 1666

Who cannot be crushed with a plot?

CHAPTER
10

I WASN'T EXPECTING SO MANY
spaniels.

Tom and I shuffled nervously as Lord Ashcombe ushered us into the king's private study, on the second floor of the palace. It was bright and spacious, the rounded window providing a fantastic view of London over the Thames. We could even see the Tower of London's turrets from here, all the way across the city, peeking through the faint morning mist.

Near the window was a grand desk of mahogany, where a servant stood rearranging several papers into neat piles. By the coal fire were four chairs upholstered in velvet, a second servant waiting behind them with a bottle of wine on a tray. The king sat in front of the fire, looking with bemusement at a letter.

And everywhere, everywhere, were dogs. A dozen spaniels romped about the room, snuffling through the rugs. One pup lay on his back in Charles's lap, squirming happily and gnawing at the king's fingers as he scratched idly at the dog's belly. The others came running from all corners of the room as we entered, tails wagging, weaving playfully through our feet.

"Boys! Welcome. Join me," the king said, sounding in a pleasant mood indeed.

We hesitated. As commoners, we weren't allowed to sit in the king's presence.

Charles waved away our worries. "Sit, sit," he commanded. "No one will see you but Richard here, and he knows how to keep a secret."

Tom and I exchanged a glance. The king hadn't considered the servants, even as the man behind him stepped forward to place glasses of wine on the small tables between the chairs. *No one ever pays attention to servants,* Sally had said once, a fact that had nearly spelled our doom in Paris.

But we did as he wished. The chairs *were* awfully comfortable. Two of the spaniels immediately sprang up, front paws on Tom's thighs; he ruffled their ears in delight. An older dog placed her graying muzzle on my leg and looked at me with hopeful eyes.

"That's Barbara," the king said. "She won't leave until you pet her. Of course, she won't leave after you pet her either, so there you are." I scratched Barbara's neck as Charles turned to Lord Ashcombe and held up the letter. "Guess who wrote to me."

"The tailor, demanding you pay your bills?" Lord Ashcombe said.

"Odd's fish, you've a cheek this morning," Charles said, more in amusement than outrage. "It's from La Grande Mademoiselle."

Lord Ashcombe looked surprised. "What does she want?"

"How would I know? I'm hardly going to read it."

"Sire," Lord Ashcombe said reprovingly.

"Did you boys meet La Grande Mademoiselle in Paris?" When we shook our heads, the king said, "Anne-Marie-Louise d'Orléans, duchesse de Montpensier. Dreadful woman. My mother kept trying to arrange a marriage with her while I was in France. She was annoyingly persistent."

The king gave me a sidelong glance, a smile playing about his lips. Clearly, he wanted me to ask. "How did you get out of it, Your Majesty?"

He could barely suppress a grin. "Tell him, Richard."

"Oh, for the love of the holy," Lord Ashcombe said.

"Tell him, tell him. The boy wants to know."

Lord Ashcombe sighed. "He pretended he didn't know French."

"For two years!" The king burst into laughter, startling the spaniel on his lap. "She would come to me, and I'd just look blankly at her as she tried to make conversation. She thought I was singularly ill bred. Said it right in front of my face! Ha-ha-ha!"

"Didn't she ever see you talk to anyone else?" I said.

"Of course! I'd be right in the middle of a conversation—then she'd join us and suddenly I'd lose the power of speech. Never figured it out! As dim as a candle in the countryside, that woman. And no conception of humor. Literally couldn't understand what a joke was." He shook his head. "Make no mistake, boys: No decision will bring more happiness to your home, or more grief, than whom you choose for a wife. So choose wisely."

Suddenly he sat up. The dog squirmed from his lap onto

the rug, where it gnawed on the king's shoe instead. "I just had a wonderful idea." He pointed at me just as I was taking a drink. "You should marry Sally!"

I sprayed wine everywhere.

The dogs seemed to think this was great fun. So did the king. "Wine in the stomach, not the rug, surely," he said.

Tom slapped both his hands over his mouth. I tried not to look at him.

"S-sire?" I stammered, wiping my lips.

"Why not marry Sally?" he insisted. "She's brave, loyal, clever—and let's face it, extremely easy on the eyes." He leaned in conspiratorially. "You know, as her guardian, it's my duty to arrange a suitable marriage. I could provide a very reasonable dowry, given the right fellow."

A sound escaped from Tom, which was either him being strangled, or stifling a laugh.

"I . . . er . . . it's . . ." I couldn't seem to find any way out of this. "I'm an apprentice," I said finally.

"So?"

"I'm not allowed to get married. Until my apprenticeship is over."

"Odd's fish. I hadn't thought of that. Well, you'd best hurry it up, then. Sally's certain to attract suitors at Court, and I won't wait forever. What about you, Thomas?"

Tom stared in horror. "Me?"

"Surely you must have some girl who's sweet on you."

He turned red as an apple. "Oh, no. No, no. No."

I smiled at Tom. My turn. "He's being modest, sire. You should have seen the way the maids in Paris fawned over him."

The king nodded. "How well I remember. Like vultures, they are."

"There is a girl here in London who likes him," I said. "Dorothy, the innkeeper's daughter, who lives across from my shop. She's been trying to catch Tom for some time."

"Sounds excellent. Is she pretty?"

"Very," I said, "but maybe a bit . . . aggressive."

"How so?"

"Imagine a bear trying to open a jar of honey. And Tom's the jar."

The king doubled over in laughter. Tom buried his face in his hands. Lord Ashcombe just sighed and shook his head.

Charles wiped away tears and patted Tom on the knee. "Ah, you two. Have no fear, Thomas, I'll find you someone suitable."

"Perhaps, sire," Lord Ashcombe said, "the betrothals can wait. Until the boys are no longer fourteen, at least."

"Odd's fish. I keep forgetting how young you are. You've just served me so well." He clapped his hands. "Which brings me to the point. I promised you gifts."

He turned serious. "You three, Sally included, accepted great danger in traveling to Paris, with no idea whom or what you might face. You did this at my request, and yet asked for nothing in return. You saved the life of my sister, Minette, which means more to me than my own—which you have saved, even so.

"I considered giving you titles, but that wouldn't fit my plans for you at the moment. Therefore, instead, I have decided to provide you with a pension. Six hundred pounds per annum, divided between the three."

Tom swayed in his chair, white with shock. I went dizzy myself, a low buzzing filling my head.

A pension?

Of *six hundred pounds*?

That meant Tom, Sally, and I would each be given two hundred pounds, every year.

A journeyman apothecary could hope to make a shilling a day. That worked out to around fifteen pounds a year.

The king would be giving us—each, giving us *each*—thirteen times that.

Forever.

It was well known Charles was generous with money. He'd given a similar sum to the family who'd helped him escape the country fifteen years ago, when Cromwell's troops had been hunting for his head. And yet this . . . I could barely breathe.

Tom stared, slack-jawed. "But you already gave me this hat."

Again the king doubled over with laughter. "Odd's fish, Thomas. I must invite you to all my parties."

Head still buzzing, I asked, "Does Sally know?"

"She was informed last night," Charles said, "upon her arrival at Berkshire House. I would have liked to have told her myself, but circumstances didn't permit."

I wished I'd been there to see it. She should be here, with us; she deserved to be.

And as that occurred to me, even dizzy as I was, it struck me as odd. Telling Sally about the pension could have waited a day. He could have brought her here this morning, told us all together.

But he hadn't. What's more, we'd been told there

weren't any spare quarters. Yet an irate knight had been displaced from his parlor to accommodate Tom and me. The same could have been done for Sally, if Charles had wished it. Which meant . . .

"You don't want Sally at Whitehall," I said suddenly.

The king looked at me sharply but said nothing.

Barbara the spaniel decided she wanted more than a scratch and climbed carefully into my lap. I stroked her fur, long and soft. "Is it because of Mary's murder?" I wondered aloud. "No, it can't be. Not alone. There must have been something else."

Now Charles looked at Lord Ashcombe.

The King's Warden shrugged. "You wanted him sticking his nose in."

"Clearly, I was right," the king said, and he nodded for Lord Ashcombe to tell me.

Ashcombe dismissed the two servants, shutting the door behind them. Then he spoke.

"There have been *two* murders," he said quietly. "Another servant girl was found in the Thames, the day before we returned to London. She'd been stabbed in the back, like Mary, but since she was fished out east of the Tower, no one imagined the murder had happened in the palace. It was assumed she'd gone to market and fallen afoul of thieves. Given yesterday's circumstances, it's fair to assume the deaths are connected—that she was killed here, and her body dumped in the river."

"Was it done with the same type of blade?" Tom asked nervously.

"No blade was found in the body." Lord Ashcombe shrugged. "Could have washed out in the Thames."

I wasn't sure if it was appropriate to bring up here, but I did anyway. "There was a letter waiting for me at Blackthorn," I began, and the king nodded.

"Richard already told me," he said. "That fits in well with my plans."

"Sire?"

"I want you to meet someone today."

"Of course, sire." I looked from him to Lord Ashcombe. "May I ask whom?"

The king smiled. "Your new master."

CHAPTER
11

I DREW A BREATH. "MY ... NEW MASTER?"

"It's clear the Apothecaries' Guild was never going to arrange it," Charles said. "So I decided to take care of it myself."

I didn't know what to say. In a way, this was an even bigger shock than the pension.

My stomach churned. Part of me had wished for this to happen. To have a new master. To be back in the workshop as an apprentice. To return to the life I'd once known. The life I'd never imagined at Cripplegate, the life I'd discovered I never wanted to leave.

And yet . . . it wasn't just being an apothecary's

apprentice I wanted. It was being Master Benedict's.

And I could never return to that.

I'd known this day was coming, of course—with no master, the guild would never let me take the test to become an apothecary—but now that it was here, I couldn't control my nerves. Who was this new man? What was he like? How could he—how could *anyone*—ever replace my true master?

The king had one answer for me, at least. "Woodrow Kirby is his name. Do you know him?"

I shook my head.

"One of my private apothecaries." A pair of spaniels vied for the king's attention; he settled the squabble by putting them both on his lap. "He's served me since my return."

Lord Ashcombe opened the door and spoke to the servants outside. A moment later, Woodrow Kirby, apothecary, entered the room.

He looked to be in his late fifties. He was an average-size man, with a bit of a belly, heavy-lidded eyes, and sagging jowls. He wore a long, black wig, and his clothes hung loose on his frame.

I'd already placed Barbara on the floor and stood, heart hammering in my chest. Tom stood automatically beside me, still holding one of the dogs.

The apothecary bowed from the waist. "Your Majesty."

"Master Kirby. This is the boy I was telling you about."

Kirby looked me up and down. What he was hoping to see, I didn't know. His face didn't betray any feeling. "Rowe, is it?"

"Yes, Master," I said. My voice cracked, which left me mortified. "Christopher."

The apothecary glanced over at the king. "With His Majesty's permission . . . ?"

The king nodded.

"List the four humors," Kirby said.

So. It was to be a test. "Blood, phlegm, yellow bile, black bile," I answered.

"Odd's fish, even I know that," the king said. "Ask him something hard."

Kirby thought for a moment. "Describe briefly anything you know about how to produce spirits of salt."

"Um . . . by Valentinus's process? Or Glauber's, Master?"

He blinked at me. Charles covered a smile. *The king is showing me off,* I realized. I felt rather like one of his spaniels.

"Glauber's," the apothecary said.

"Heat salt in the presence of oil of vitriol," I answered. "Distill and condense the vapor."

"Harder, Kirby, harder," the king urged. I wished he'd stop.

The apothecary thought a little longer this time. Then he said, "List as many ingredients as you can that are used in the production of the Venice treacle."

This *was* a difficult question—namely because Venice treacle had sixty-four ingredients. Except not only had Venice treacle been a specialty of Master Benedict's, but, after the trouble during the plague, Magistrate Aldebourne had contracted me to produce as much of it as I could. I knew this answer cold.

I began with the most famous ingredient: snake venom. *"Viperinorum,"* I said. *"Trochiscorum scilliticorum, hedichroi radicum gentianae, acori veri, valerianae . . ."*

I continued, the king grinning openly as Kirby stared in amazement. I think I missed a few—I lost count somewhere around ingredient thirty—but I'm not sure the apothecary noticed.

"What did I tell you?" Charles said proudly.

Kirby looked me up and down again, this time with a new scrutiny. "You were Blackthorn's apprentice."

"Yes, Master," I said.

"That explains a lot," he muttered.

"Well, Master Kirby?" the king said.

"You do understand, sire, he may need to make appearances at my laboratory?"

"He'll be at your disposal as necessary."

"And he'll still have to pass a final exam to become a journeyman."

Charles smiled. "I don't think that will be a problem."

"No," Kirby said. "I don't suppose it will. Very well, sire. I accept."

Charles nodded his thanks. With a bow to the king, and a final glance in my direction, Kirby left the room.

I was thoroughly confused. I had no idea what that last exchange was about, and the apothecary's abrupt departure left me wondering what I was supposed to do. I'd assumed I would follow him, but the king hadn't given me permission to leave.

"Should I go with Master Kirby, sire?" I said.

The king shook his head. "Richard will look after you. Always a delight, boys."

And so we were dismissed. I was still reeling; it took a jerk of the head from Lord Ashcombe—and an elbow in my side from Tom—to get me moving. The spaniels stayed behind.

"My lord . . . ?" I began as soon as we were in the hall.

Lord Ashcombe raised a hand to silence me. There was a pair of guards by the door, and servants standing farther down the passageway. He wanted to wait until we were alone.

Once the three of us had found an empty corridor, Lord Ashcombe stopped. He spoke in a low voice. "Tomorrow, Kirby will notify the Apothecaries' Guild that he has taken you as an apprentice. If anyone asks, you will identify him as your master."

"I thought he *was* my master," I said, more confused than ever.

"No. That's just for show."

"Then . . . who is?"

"You are being apprenticed to Alexander Walsingham, 1st Earl Walsingham."

I didn't recognize the name. "Is he another of His Majesty's private apothecaries?"

"No," Lord Ashcombe said. "He's the king's personal spymaster."

CHAPTER
12

I STARED AT LORD ASHCOMBE, stunned. "You want me to become a *spy*?"

"Haven't we had this discussion before? You already are a spy, Christopher. This just makes it official."

I didn't know what to say. My whole world was turning upside down. I felt like I'd lost all control of my life.

Then again, maybe control was just an illusion. In Cripplegate, I'd done whatever I was told. With Master Benedict, I'd done that, too. Following orders was, after all, the role of an apprentice. Learn, practice, cook, clean. Run errands. Whatever the master says.

Yet it never felt like that with Master Benedict. I'd loved

being an apprentice—*his* apprentice. He'd taught me and cared for me, and I'd adored the work, even when the days were long. I'd *wanted* to become an apothecary.

When he was murdered, and I was left on my own, I'd been heartbroken—and I'd also been free. No one around to tell me what to do. I'd have given every ounce of freedom to have him back. But he wasn't coming back. He lived only in my heart.

And being free didn't bring any opportunities. I'd still learned, practiced, cooked, cleaned, ran errands. Without a master, none of that would have got me any closer to my dreams.

Now I was supposed to become a spy? Again, someone else was making my decisions for me. It wasn't the apprentice's place to question. But I found myself questioning anyway.

What if I didn't want this?

I said none of it aloud. Nonetheless, Lord Ashcombe seemed to understand the struggle going on inside.

"You have the right to refuse," he said. "I told you before you went to Paris, you are not a slave. But His Majesty needs you. And, whatever you say, this sort of thing is what you're best at.

"You will still be an apothecary. As Kirby said, you'll need to make appearances in his laboratory, take examinations. And Blackthorn will remain your shop. You'll just be, in secret, this other thing as well."

I wasn't sure about any of it, not at all. But if I could still be an apothecary . . . it made me feel a little better. "Yes, my lord."

"Now, about Walsingham. He's strange. Dealing with him requires patience. But he's loyal, and brilliant, and an exceptional spy."

Nerves fluttered in my gut. "Yes, my lord."

I looked over at Tom. He seemed just as stunned as I was, by everything. But he wasn't about to meet the king's chief spymaster. He gave me a look of sympathy, which was pretty much all he could do.

And then we were there. Somewhere inside the maze that was Whitehall, Lord Ashcombe stopped at a door and motioned to it.

I knocked. A quiet, baritone voice said, "Enter."

I took a deep breath and went inside.

CHAPTER
13

THE SPYMASTER'S OFFICE WAS narrow and cramped, with no windows. A desk near the far wall had been placed to face the door, so anyone sitting behind it could see who came in.

Alexander Walsingham, 1st Earl Walsingham, was not at his desk. He sat, instead, on one of two plain wooden chairs in front of it, angled slightly toward each other. The spymaster was younger than I'd expected, maybe in his late thirties, and possibly not even that. His wig lay on the desk, revealing a head of close-cropped blond hair. He was lean, not particularly tall, and somewhat plain looking. Not the sort of man one might remember in a crowd—which I supposed was good for a spy.

If I hadn't heard him say "enter," I'd have thought he was having a nap. He was just sitting there, eyes closed. Without opening them, he motioned to the chair beside him.

"Sit," he said in that same quiet baritone.

I did. And I waited.

Walsingham made no more gestures, said no more words. He simply sat there in silence, again looking to all the world as if he were fast asleep.

Was I supposed to acknowledge him? Introduce myself? Start the conversation?

I opened my mouth to speak but stopped. Lord Ashcombe had said the man was odd—but he'd also said dealing with the spymaster required patience.

Was that a hint?

I didn't know. But if Walsingham was to be my master, it was up to him to decide what I should do. So I just sat there and waited.

Minutes passed. At first, my mind raced. There's a strange sort of pressure, sitting with a stranger, no one saying anything. Should I disturb him? Keep silent? Sing a song? Sally could sing wonderfully; where was she when I needed her? *Safe in Berkshire House,* I thought, *away from all the murders.* But as more time passed—I swear, it had to be approaching an hour—I grew bored. Trying not to fidget, I studied the room.

There was a bookshelf by the door; oddly, none of the books' spines were labeled. A few paintings hung on the walls. There was an Oriental rug under our feet, too large for the floor; one edge curled a few inches where it ran out of room to stretch. The desk was free of all papers; nothing on top but a ticking clock and the spymaster's discarded wig. A faint scent of mint filled the room. I couldn't tell from where it was coming.

Eventually, I ran out of things to study. So I turned my mind to the cipher in yesterday's message. And the key I still hadn't discovered.

Remember Paris, the letter had said. I'd already tried the obvious words, and none of them had worked. So what was I forgetting?

I'd just begun to run over the whole trip in my mind. Then I noticed: Walsingham's eyes were open.

And he was staring at me.

His gaze was penetrating, unsettling. It was like he was looking right through me. I almost said "Master?" just to still my nerves, but I managed to clamp my mouth shut.

"Keep your eyes fixed on me," he said, quiet as ever.

I'm not sure I could have pulled away, even if I'd wanted to.

"The door you entered," he said. "On one side is a bookshelf. What is on the other?"

Another test, I realized.

And this one even more important.

I searched my memory. "A painting."

"Of?"

"A . . . naval battle. Naval siege, I mean. Ships, attacking a city."

"How many ships?"

How many *ships*? "Uh . . ." I closed my eyes, tried to remember.

There were three in the foreground, tilting against the waves. Three more behind them. Then one closer to the city . . . no, wait. Two. That made . . .

"Eight," I said.

"And what city are they attacking?"

How on earth was I supposed to know that? "I . . . I'm sorry, I don't know."

"If you had to guess?"

"Um . . . Bilbao?"

The spymaster tilted his head, curious. "What makes you say that?"

"Well . . . the city looks Dutch, but the ships are English, and the painting was clearly done years ago, probably during the war with Spain. Since the painting is in the Dutch style, I figured the artist used his own memory to create a city he'd never been to. Like how painters put the faces of people they know as saints, or whatever. I know we've attacked Spanish cities, so I chose the closest port, which is Bilbao. I think."

"Interesting. You may look."

The first thing I did was count the ships. Yes, there were eight . . . Oh no. "There are nine," I said, disappointed. "There's another mast sticking up behind the ship on the left."

"Yes."

"May I ask what city it is?"

"I have no idea."

I blinked. "So there's no right answer?"

"There often isn't." Walsingham shifted in his chair. "The purpose of my question, then: Can you understand it?"

If there was no right answer . . . then the answer wasn't what mattered. Instead . . . "It was about me," I said. "What—or rather *how*—I think."

He nodded. "You are acceptable. You may inform Ashcombe of this."

Was I being dismissed? I began to rise. "Yes, Master."

"Never call me that."

I flushed. "Sorry, Ma—uh . . . my lord. I thought—"

"I *am* your master," Walsingham said, "and the title brings no shame. Nonetheless, you must avoid calling me so, even in private.

"Keep this in your mind always: Our association is to be secret. So, from this day forward, your only master is Woodrow Kirby, apothecary. If you must refer to me publicly—and you should avoid this wherever possible— refer to me only by my title. I am Lord Walsingham, or His Lordship, the Earl."

"I understand, my lord."

"Of course," he said, "your role will not remain a secret. Nothing ever does. But, at the very least, we can avoid hastening the discovery. Tell me about your mission in Paris."

His abrupt change of topic threw me. "I wrote some letters to Lord Ashcombe—"

"I read them. I wish to hear the story directly from you."

I'd already begun to recall my trip, while I'd been waiting for Walsingham to speak. Now I told the tale out loud, beginning with the attempt on Minette's life in Oxford, up to the execution of the traitors outside the Bastille, and the discovery that Rémi—the head servant at Maison Chastellain, and who called himself the Raven—was behind it all. When I finished, the spymaster studied me.

"You are an excellent storyteller," he said.

"Um . . . thank you, my lord."

"And you are an equally excellent liar."

CHAPTER
14

THE SPYMASTER'S EYES BURNED
into me.

"My lord?" I said, flustered. "I swear, everything I told you really happened—"

"I believe that," he said, still quiet. "And yet, your story does not add up. There is something you are *not* telling me. Your lie is a lie of omission."

I wasn't sure how to answer that. Because he was right.

The one thing I'd left out of my letters, the one thing only Tom and Sally knew, was that the Templars weren't dead. Their ancient order still existed, after all these centuries, operating behind the scenes, in secret, to protect the world from descending into chaos. After we'd discovered this, I'd promised a Templar priest, Father Bernard, that I wouldn't spread the word. And I hadn't.

"My lord . . ." I had no idea what I was going to say. So I was relieved when Walsingham raised his hand to silence me.

"It is a spy's job—*your* job—to keep secrets," he said. "I will not begrudge you that. But you must understand: You work now for His Majesty. Whatever personal secrets you hold, you may not keep, if they threaten the king. Is that clear?"

"Yes, my lord."

"Then I will ask you: Do you know of anything that is a danger to His Majesty?"

The Templars were no threat to Charles, I was certain. In fact, they'd told me the opposite: They'd often worked to thwart plots against the French king, Louis XIV, even if they hadn't always succeeded. So my answer could be true.

"No, my lord."

"You received a message. May I see it?"

Again, that abrupt change of topic threw me. I reached into my doublet to hand him the letter I'd found in my shop.

He studied it carefully, silent.

An oath was made, a promise sworn
To those who wished to bind him.

But he returned, and offered scorn
And so they come to find him.

You will know the key when you see
the truth. Remember Paris.

MOIURHJBXAMGXBHBLL

He stared at a blank space on the wall, as if he were looking out of a window, instead of at empty plaster. He remained that way for a few minutes. Then he spoke.

"Do you know what the riddle means?"

"The first part? Um . . . no," I said.

"You hesitate."

"Well . . . I have an idea. My friend Tom suggested it, actually. I think it might refer to the king."

"Why?"

I went through our discussion from yesterday. "At first, I thought it might be about me. Because the letter was left for me, and I'd just returned, like it says. But I haven't broken any oaths"—not even now, when Walsingham had called me out for lying about Paris—"so I don't think it fits. His Majesty also returned, when he got the throne back in 1660. And there have been two murders in the palace already. I don't know what promise he's supposed to have scorned, but I'm guessing it relates to those deaths."

The spymaster remained silent, staring at the wall.

"Do you think it refers to the king, my lord?" I said.

"Yes."

"Whom do you think is the threat?"

"I'm not going to tell you."

That was unexpected. "All right."

He turned back to meet my eyes. "I stay silent because of something critically important you must understand." He spread his hands. "This—this moment here—is the most dangerous time in an investigation."

I'd figured the most dangerous time was when the bullets started flying. "Why is that, my lord?"

"The human mind," he said, "is exceptional at recognizing patterns. So good, in fact, that when there *are* no patterns, we invent them to fill the gaps. Once a man's mind is fixed on what he believes is the truth, nothing else can be real. If he finds evidence that supports his theory, then he is correct. If he finds evidence that refutes his theory, does he rethink his beliefs? Very rarely. Instead, he dismisses the evidence, or finds some way to twist it so it will fit his view of the world. He simply refuses to see.

"I have a theory. I believe it is correct. But I do not *know* it. So I will not pollute your mind. I suspect more evidence will come to light over the next few days. Form your own theory, then come to me. We will see if we agree."

I couldn't really argue with that. Not knowing what he thought was frustrating, yes, but his reasoning made a lot of sense. In fact, the spymaster had begun to remind me of Master Benedict—and not just because he could be a bit strange sometimes, too. He'd also cautioned me against jumping to conclusions.

"What about the cipher?" Walsingham said.

"I'm pretty sure it's Vigenère," I said, "but I haven't been able to figure out the key."

"You're familiar with Vigenère, then?"

"Yes, my lord. My master taught me. Master Benedict, I mean."

"I understood. The key, or the message—can you tell me anything about them?"

The way he asked made me think he already knew

something. "No, my lord . . . Can you?"

"Yes." I half expected him to say again he wouldn't tell me what. Instead, he said, softly as ever, "Sit at my desk."

I did.

"In the drawer to your right, you will find a quill, ink, and paper. I want you to do an exercise."

Another test? Inwardly, I sighed, but I did as he commanded. I also took the paper with the Vigenère square out from under my apothecary sash.

He looked at it briefly, then nodded in approval. "I want you to encode a simple message. A single word: 'the.'"

I felt like saying *That's it?* But dutifully, I wrote it down. "And the key?"

"The same word."

"'The' again?"

"Correct."

I wrote it out, the key over the message.

THE

THE

"Encode it," the spymaster said. "And do it out loud."

This seemed awfully pointless, but, title or not, he

was my master now. "To encipher something," I said, "we start with the first letter of the key, *T*, in the row, and the first letter of the message, *T*, in the column. Then go down and across, and we get . . . *M*."

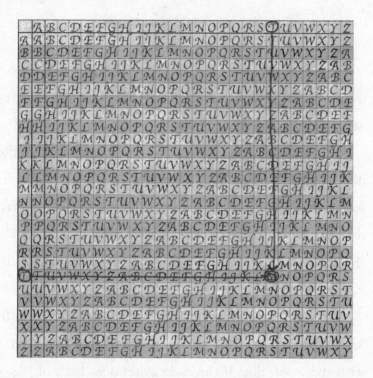

"Next we match the second letters," I said. "*H* with *H* gets . . . *O*. Finally, *E* with *E* makes . . . *I*. So all together, we get *MOI* . . . wait."

THE

THE

"MOI," I said, surprised. "That's the first three letters of the code!"

M O I U R H J B X A M G X B H B L L

"So it is," the spymaster said. "And we see our mystery messenger has made a mistake."

Walsingham stood and came around to my side of the desk. "Vigenère is said to be unbreakable," he said. *"Le chiffre indéchiffrable,* they call it: the indecipherable cipher. So far, that has proved to be correct. But even with an unbreakable code, we may find clues. For where the code succeeds, sometimes *people* fail.

"It is not uncommon to start a message with the word 'the.' It is also not uncommon to use a key that begins with the word 'the.' If the codemaker does both of these, then the first three letters of the message will always read the same: *M, O, I.* And he will have given away part of what he is trying to hide."

"How did you discover this?" I said, amazed.

"I have spent my lifetime studying codes. Much failed

hunting, a few gems unearthed. At any rate, knowing something about the key may prompt the decipherer to realize . . ."

He went on talking, but I wasn't listening. I stared at the message, and the code, and the exercise I'd just finished. Then I sprang from my seat.

"I know," I said. "I know what the key is."

CHAPTER
15

THE SPYMASTER STUDIED MY FACE.
"Do tell."

"It's here," I said. "Right here in the message. I can't believe I didn't see it."

I turned the letter I'd received toward him.

"The instruction, before the code. It says, 'You will know the key when you see the truth. Remember Paris.' I thought they were talking about what happened in France: the assassins, or their search for the lost Templar treasure, something like that. But when we were in Paris, trying to solve the riddles, Tom pointed something out.

"He noticed that for all the old clues the Templars left,

the solution was always *literal*. That is, you'd think the puzzles were confusing, but if you read each clue exactly as written, you'd understand what they really meant.

"So let's do the same. Take this line literally. You will know the key *when you see the truth*."

And I circled the words.

You will know the key when you see (the truth.) Remember Paris.

"When you see . . . 'the truth.'" Walsingham raised an eyebrow. "Fascinating."

He motioned for me to try it. I wrote the code out, the key *THETRUTH* above it. Then I got to work. Even after only half the code, I knew I'd found what we were looking for.

THETRUTHTHETRUTHTH

MOIURHJBXAMGXBHBLL

THEBANQUETINGHOUSE

"The Banqueting House," I said.

"Do you know where that is?" Walsingham asked.

"It's part of the palace. Just outside." I frowned. "But what does it mean?"

"I suppose you'll have to go find out."

I looked at him, surprised. "You're not going to take over?"

"Why would I?"

"Well . . . you're the m—you're in charge. I just thought . . ."

"This message was not meant for me," the spymaster said.

"You still solved it."

"No. I recognized a pattern, and educated you. The solution was in your head, not mine. Only you knew the secret of Paris." Walsingham pushed the letter toward me. "Whoever sent you this appears to be trying to help. They have chosen you as their contact. I see no reason to replace you. I suspect they would not even permit it.

"If you need my assistance, you may come to me, any time, day or night. I will not be here today; there are matters I must attend to at the docks, regarding the war with the Dutch. But I shall return this evening. If you have found something, visit me then.

"Otherwise: go to the Banqueting House, apprentice. And do your job."

CHAPTER
16

"WELL?" LORD ASHCOMBE SAID.

I'd spied him coming out of his office. Trailing behind him, Tom was frowning. He looked troubled.

"Lord Walsingham told me to inform you I was acceptable," I said.

Lord Ashcombe snorted. "Consider that high praise. What did you think?"

"You were right. He's brilliant."

He'd been right about the other thing, too: The spymaster *was* strange. The meeting had left my head spinning. But I think I liked him. I might not be allowed to say the title in public, but I was starting to feel like he'd make a good master.

I showed them our solution to the cipher, and explained what Walsingham had said about my going to the Banqueting House. Lord Ashcombe agreed that made sense. "Keep me apprised of anything you learn. And belt your weapons on again; there's a murderer about. Unless you're meeting the king, you stay armed."

"Will we need a key?"

"To the Banqueting House? It won't be locked. Nothing is, in the palace."

"Is that a good idea, my lord?" Tom said.

Lord Ashcombe shook his head, frustrated. "Servants are in and out of rooms all day long," he pointed out. "Locked doors would grind the palace to a halt. You'd need to leave keys everywhere."

Which would obviously defeat the purpose. "What should we do if we need to leave Whitehall?" I said.

"Just go. The guards will have instructions to let you pass." He handed us a coin purse. "For any expenses. And if you need to go far, head to the stables. I've ordered a pair of horses to be set aside for you."

Tom and I exchanged a glance. Our own mounts? How our world had changed!

"You're in service to the king now," Lord Ashcombe

reminded us. "You have resources. If they help protect His Majesty, I expect you to use them. Just don't forget: What you do in his name reflects on the Crown. You've been given an enormous amount of trust. Don't betray it."

"We won't, my lord," we promised, and Lord Ashcombe walked away.

Tom and I headed toward our quarters for our weapons—in at least what we thought was the right direction. I wasn't paying much attention, trying instead to quiet the fluttering in my gut. That enormous weight I'd felt on our way to Paris had returned.

It seemed to weigh on Tom, too. Or maybe it was something else. He'd looked troubled when I'd spotted him with Lord Ashcombe. Now that frown had crept onto his brow again.

"Is everything all right?" I said.

"Hmm?"

"I asked if you're all right."

"Yes. Fine." He seemed surprised.

"What were you two talking about?" I said.

"Who?"

"You and Lord Ashcombe. You were in his office."

"Oh. Nothing." He paused. "I mean, training."

"Training?"

"Yes. You know, while we were staying with the King's Men, I got to train all the time. Lord Ashcombe asked if I—I mean, *I* asked Lord Ashcombe—if I could still train with them now that we're home. I thought maybe even with Sir William Leech. You remember him."

Of course I remembered him. He was Tom's first sword master. We'd spent two weeks with him on the road to Paris. "And?"

"And what? Oh—he said maybe. He'd look into it."

"That would be great," I said.

"Yeah." Tom stopped. "I think our room is this way."

He walked on. I followed him, puzzled, confused, and hurt.

Tom had just lied to me.

CHAPTER 17

I DIDN'T UNDERSTAND IT.

Tom didn't always approve of the things I did, especially when they involved fire. Sometimes I annoyed him. Rarely, I made him cross. In Paris, he'd been absolutely furious with me for a time.

But he never, ever lied. Not to me. If anything, I wished sometimes he'd keep his feelings to himself.

Yet he'd lied to me, just then. I could tell. It was in his face, the way he hadn't wanted to look at me while we were speaking.

It wasn't just the lie, either. Something in his manner made him seem a little sad, though I wasn't sure what.

At first, I wondered if it was because he missed his family. He'd been so looking forward to seeing his little sisters again, and his spirits had sunk awfully low when he'd learned he wouldn't. His family had been staying on a boat moored in the center of the Thames to avoid the plague. By now, the death count had fallen, from thousands a week to a mere dozen. But the scare his mother had had when she thought Tom was infected had left her hysterical. According to the last letter she'd sent, she was refusing to let any of her children off the boat until there were absolutely no more cases.

But if it was his sisters he was sad about, he'd tell me. Him keeping a secret couldn't be good. I wanted to press him on it. And yet, I was afraid to ask. If he'd gone so far as to lie . . . I didn't think I'd like the answer.

I followed him silently, wishing I was a little more brave.

Tom found our room eventually. The first thing I did was slip the map of the palace under my apothecary sash; it was clear we needed it. Then we armed ourselves: me with my twin pistols; Tom with Eternity, his Templar sword, strapped to his back. As usual, he wrapped a cloth around the moonstone pommel and gilded hilt to hide its craftsmanship. It was a blade fit for a king, not a commoner.

Bridget ran around the room madly on our return. I picked her up. Normally, this would quiet her, but she fussed in my hands. "What is with you?" I said.

She cooed, which didn't explain anything. "Restless to be home," Tom suggested, which is what I'd thought yesterday, but she hadn't been this agitated last night. I supposed there was no harm in letting her out. When we entered the courtyard, I released her. She flapped her wings and flew off into the sky.

The Banqueting House was across the courtyard, between the entry to the palace and the Holbein Gate. Despite its name, it was rarely used for dining. Instead, it was a presence chamber, where His Majesty would receive visiting ambassadors or hold other public functions. I wondered how the king felt about the place; seventeen years ago, his father, Charles I, had been executed right in front of it in the street.

The House was a later addition to the palace, built some forty years ago by one of our greatest architects, Inigo Jones. The outside was simple and elegant, seven windows wide, with three central bays and columns on the upper and lower stories. Its face was a mix of colors: pink, honey, and white, created from three different kinds of stone.

As Lord Ashcombe had said, the Banqueting House was unlocked and empty. Inside was one large room, designed as a perfect double cube, 110 feet long, fifty-five feet wide and high. Along both sides of the hall, pillars rose from the floor up to the gallery overlooking the main space. When Charles did dine here, the gallery was where the commoners would stand, to watch our king as he ate.

Tom's voice echoed in the emptiness. "So what are we looking for?"

The letter hadn't said. "I'm not sure."

I studied the ceiling. Between the gilded beams were nine magnificent canvases, all by the Flemish painter Sir Peter Paul Rubens. The scenes were a celebration of the life of James I, grandfather to our king.

"Look for marks on the walls," I said, "or something left behind, out of place. Anything out of the ordinary."

"Everything we're doing is out of the ordinary," Tom grumbled, and I couldn't really disagree with that.

Nothing jumped out at me on the ground floor. Below the hall was an undercroft, but before we delved into the dungeon, I figured we might as well check out the gallery overhead.

We went upstairs. Tom took the left side; I went around

to the right. A balustrade ringed the gallery, but other than that, there didn't appear to be anything up here. I studied the floor below, wondering if I might spot something from a higher perspective. When that offered nothing, I looked up again at the canvases.

Directly overhead was a painting of Hercules, wielding a club, stomping on a woman holding a snake, who was supposed to represent Envy. On the other side, the Greek goddess Minerva plunged a spear into another woman, who represented Ignorance.

I really hoped the paintings weren't the clue. We'd had enough trouble with one in Paris. And there were nine of them here, hanging a dozen feet over our heads. Lord Ashcombe had said we had a lot of leeway investigating for the king, but I didn't think anyone would be pleased if we started ripping Rubens off the ceiling.

Well, we still had the grottoes beneath the Banqueting House to search. I was just about to tell Tom I was going downstairs when he called to me. His voice reverberated in the hall.

"Christopher."

I went around to his side. He was standing at the far end, staring at the railing atop the balustrade, right at the corner. He pointed.

A letter lay folded on top of the rail. I picked it up and saw what was written on the front.

C. R.

Christopher Rowe. Left for me, where no one else was likely to find it.

The back was sealed, a featureless circle stamped in red wax. Just like the letter I'd found in Blackthorn.

I cracked the seal. Then Tom and I huddled by the window to read the message inside.

CHAPTER 18

TOM STARED AT IT, CONFUSED.

"What is this?"

> *Saints defend these ancient walls,*
> *Saints we hope will save,*
>
> *Visit them in hallowed halls,*
> *And pray upon his grave.*
>
> *la ruota dell'italiano*

B s m v & h c t c q q t d k d & l x

"Another puzzle," I said, excited. "But I *know* this one."

"The rhyme?"

"The code. I know what it is. I need— We have to go back to Blackthorn."

"Why?"

"There's a device," I said. "A cipher device. Master Benedict has one—had one. We need to find it."

"Oh," Tom said, pleased. "We'll get to take the horses—"

I clapped my hand over his mouth.

Below us, the door to the Banqueting House squeaked open. Then we heard the clop of leather heels on floor.

Quickly, I flattened myself behind the balustrade. Tom got down with me, looking puzzled.

Aren't we allowed to be here? he mouthed.

We were, but what I was doing was supposed to be a secret. I didn't want to have to explain our presence. What's more, Lord Ashcombe had said no one should be in the Banqueting House at this hour. It was an awful coincidence for someone to show up just after we'd gone in.

Unless they were here for a similar reason.

Or here for *us*.

I peeked through the rails. A man stepped into the hall.

He was at the opposite end, near the door, but I could make out his face well enough.

I'd seen him before. He was one of the men held up at the palace gate, when Lord Ashcombe and I had arrived at Whitehall during the lockdown. The taller one, with trimmed beard, gold spectacles, and an irate Scottish companion.

He took a step closer, glancing around the hall. A pistol hung from his belt. He held a letter, but this one wasn't meant for us. It was already open.

He looked around, suspicious. Then he laid his hand on the grip of his pistol.

"Hello?"

Like his companion yesterday, this man also had a Scottish accent. Tom looked at me, eyes wide. I stayed absolutely still, afraid to breathe.

The man frowned. He tried again.

"Is someone there?"

Slowly, he drew his pistol. Then he stepped closer, heels echoing in the hall. He looked around, then up at the gallery. I hoped he couldn't see us through the balustrade.

He backed away, one step, another. Then, abruptly, he spun on his heels and stalked from the Banqueting House. The door creaked and slammed behind him.

"Come on," I whispered to Tom. I ran to the windows, barely peeking my head above the sill, trying to see where the man had gone.

He strode across the courtyard, toward the main palace buildings. Suddenly he turned, looking up at the Banqueting House, eyes narrowed.

I ducked down, heart thumping. Had he spotted us?

I waited a moment. Then I crawled to a different window, farther along the gallery, and peeked out again.

I didn't know if he'd seen us, but he wasn't coming back. One of the guards had started a small fire near the entrance to the courtyard. The Scotsman was already there.

He held the letter in the flames. One corner caught fire. The man watched it burn for a moment, then dropped it.

He went inside the palace as the letter turned to ash.

CHAPTER
19

TOM LEANED AGAINST THE WALL.
"What was that about?" he said.

I wished I knew. The man had a letter, like us. Did it say the same thing? Had it told him to search the Banqueting House?

Or was it something else?

The thing that worried me most was that, unlike us, he hadn't bothered to look around. If anything, he'd acted like he was being lured into a trap.

"Maybe he's the murderer," Tom said.

"I don't know about that." I explained how I'd seen the man yesterday, outside the palace gate.

"He still could have done it," Tom insisted. "He kills Mary Brickenham, then leaves the palace right away. So he's already gone by the time she's found, and he's outside for the lockdown. That way, no one suspects him."

It was possible. Still, we couldn't be sure. The man had behaved oddly, yes, but that didn't make him a murderer. I remembered the spymaster's warning about jumping to conclusions. *When there are no patterns, we invent them to fill the gaps.*

The fact was, we didn't know anything about the Scotsman. We didn't even know who he was. I wished he hadn't burned that letter. If we knew what was in it, I had the feeling we'd understand what was happening a lot better.

Well, we could at least learn the man's name. "Lord Ashcombe saw him, too," I said. "He might know who he is."

We went looking for the King's Warden but were told he'd left Whitehall for a meeting at the docks. Probably the same one Walsingham was going to, about the war with the Dutch.

"Should we check with someone else?" Tom said.

I shook my head. "I don't want word getting around that we're asking about the man. It'll have to wait until

Lord Ashcombe's back. Besides, we're supposed to be solving this riddle."

"But if he's the killer—"

"All he did was walk into the Banqueting House. Are we supposed to tell the king that makes him guilty?"

Tom made a face. "I guess not."

"Lord Walsingham ordered me to follow the messages," I said. "I can decipher this puzzle at the shop. Besides, I want to check on Simon."

And ask him about the Raven, too, I thought.

We stopped by the stables to get our horses. Both were animals largely retired from service, the groom's apprentice told us. Tom's mount, Lightning, was an old, midnight black warhorse with a meandering blaze down his face, which looked a bit like a lightning strike—no doubt how he got his name. Lightning perked up as soon as he was taken from his stall, stamping the mud with excited energy.

I got a former carriage horse. I think the groom's apprentice was making fun of me. Not just because mine was a carriage horse—the story of my fiery accident had made its way around Whitehall, it seemed—but because my horse was a mare, a docile old girl by the name of Blossom, the farthest thing from a warhorse in the king's stable.

The apprentice smirked at me, and Tom looked embarrassed. Yes, the stable hands were definitely making sport. I sighed and checked out my new mount.

Blossom's coat was chestnut, with white socks on her hind legs. She had a star on her forehead and was going slightly gray around her lips. She looked at me with curious, intelligent eyes as I approached.

I took her reins and breathed softly into her nostrils, the way Lord Ashcombe had taught me to say hello to a horse. In return, Blossom lowered her head and nuzzled my hand with her nose. I rubbed her withers, and she stretched her neck, enjoying the scratch. So the joke was on everyone else, because I loved this gentle girl from the start.

She kept a placid pace, enjoying the walk out of Whitehall, not champing at the bit to go faster, like Lightning, who snorted as if he was ready to charge into battle. I wasn't exactly the greatest horseman, so a slower pace suited me just fine.

It was strange to see how people moved out of our way. And not just because they didn't want to get stepped on. There was a deference from the crowd, who clearly thought

I must be some kind of noble, with Tom my personal guard. Some women even curtsied as I passed, which was mildly embarrassing.

As for Tom, he did look impressive up on Lightning: broad-shouldered, wearing the king's hat, Eternity strapped to his back. Though his talking to his mount somewhat ruined the effect.

"Who's a good horse? You are. Who's the *best* horse? You are!"

"We should get Sally," I said. I wanted her to see me up on Blossom—and, well, I wanted to see her, too. "I'm sure she'd like to come with us."

Tom grinned. "I bet she would."

"Don't you start," I said, flushing. "Or I'll begin pointing out palace girls to the king."

That sobered him up. "Do you think His Majesty was serious about finding me a wife?"

"No," I said, laughing. "Would it be so bad, though? I mean, you do want to get married someday."

"Of course. But not to a court lady."

"Why not?"

"Sally told you how mean they were to her in Paris. Besides, I don't have any place in all that finery. I just want

a simple life. With a kind girl, who'll make a kind home."
He was silent for a moment. "I do think the king was right
about you, though. You should marry Sally."

"*Enough* already."

"I mean it."

To my surprise, he really did.

"Look," Tom said, "everything His Majesty said about
her was true. You'd be good together. Plus, she's got the
most important quality of all."

"What's that?"

"*I* like her," he said. "You are absolutely forbidden from
marrying a girl I don't like."

"Ha! That goes for you, too, you know."

"Naturally."

"I still think you should ask the king to introduce you
to some court ladies. If you don't want to marry them, just
say no."

Suddenly Tom looked very sad. "It's not easy to say no
to a king."

I paused. "What does that mean?"

"Nothing," he said.

He snapped the reins and rode ahead in silence.

. . .

I rode behind him for a while. I thought back to when I'd seen him exiting Lord Ashcombe's office. Why had he been in there? What were they talking about?

It occurred to me that other than the pension—and even now, I could barely believe it; a pension, it was absolutely mad—Sally and I both got additional gifts. She got to be the king's ward; I got a new master. Surely Tom deserved his own gift, too? Besides his new, beloved hat?

Had Lord Ashcombe offered him something?

And what sort of gift would make Tom sad?

I sighed. He obviously didn't want to tell me, so I just worked to cheer him up. Today, that wasn't hard to do. Apart from the fact that Tom also loved his new horse, the path to Berkshire House took us around Saint James's Park.

The green, originally a deer-hunting ground preserved for Henry VIII, had been altered by Charles to make it even more grand. Surrounded by grass and trees was a canal, forty yards wide and nearly half a mile long, upon which all sorts of waterfowl made their home. Including a bunch of white, long-necked, giant-beaked birds.

I pointed them out to Tom as we rode. "Look."

He stared, amazed. "What are those?"

"Pelicans," I said. They'd been a gift to the king from

a visiting ambassador a couple of years back; I couldn't remember from where. Master Benedict had brought me to the park that summer to see them.

Look at me now, I said in my heart. *On a horse, apprenticed to a spymaster, in service to the king. Not exactly the life I'd planned.*

Life rarely goes as planned, Master Benedict said. *The question is: Are you happy?*

Was I?

I think . . . maybe I could be. I'll always miss you. But if this business ever gets settled . . . I paused. *Tom thinks I should marry Sally.*

What do you think?

That's years away, I said.

Master Benedict sounded amused. *That's not a no.*

I shook my head. Even the angels were making fun of me.

Sally squealed when she saw us.

We were waiting in the parlor of Berkshire House while a servant went to fetch her. As we sat among the finery—portraits in gilded frames, drawers of polished walnut—it occurred to me how ordinary this sort of thing had become. And how strange that was.

Even now, all this formality to visit Sally, a Cripplegate girl. *Yes, sir, please wait in the parlor*—madness.

Sally broke through the airs by running, delighted, into our arms. Tom being closest to the entrance, she flung herself at him first. She hugged him and gave him a giant kiss on the cheek. Then she came to me. She held me longer, tighter. But she didn't give me a kiss.

Tom watched the whole thing. I narrowed my eyes at him, and he gave me an innocent look, as if to say, *I didn't say anything.* It's the thought that counts, isn't it?

Anyway. Sally looked a little flustered afterward. Though that just may have been her excitement. "Can you *believe* it?" she said. "The king's *ward*? And a *pension*? Oh— they did tell you, didn't they?"

"They did," I assured her.

"It's all so *wonderful*," she said, and she hugged me again. It felt good—and she smelled like cherries.

My face was warm. I cleared my throat. "Settling in to a life of leisure, then?"

"Oh, I don't want *that.*"

"Uncomfortable in all this luxury, are you?"

She laughed. "I wouldn't go that far. I'm *so* grateful for what the king's given us. And everyone's been so much nicer to me here than in Paris." She said the last with a genuine sigh of relief. "I've already been invited to a party. But a life of lazing around . . . I don't know. I want to be useful."

Tom and I exchanged a glance. "In that case," I said, "have we got something to tell you."

CHAPTER
20

SALLY LISTENED AS I LEANED IN and recounted the events of the last day. She was horrified by the attack on Simon, stunned at my new apprenticeships, and amazed by the letters I'd been getting. She studied the one we'd found in the Banqueting House.

"'Saints defend these ancient walls . . .' What does it mean?"

"We're off to Blackthorn to find out," I said. "Want to come?"

She stood, eyes shining. "I'll see if I can borrow a horse."

• • •

We tied our mounts outside the Missing Finger. I was just giving Blossom a good scratch before leaving when Tom said, "Look who it is."

Bridget fluttered down from the roof of my shop and ran excitedly over my boots. I picked her up, stroking her feathers as she cooed at me.

"Guess you'd rather be at home," I said, and was surprised to think, *Me, too.*

Blossom snuffled at Bridget, who eyed the horse somewhat nervously before settling down. Introductions made, I cradled Bridget in my arm, entered my shop, and got a rather rude welcome.

A club rammed into my chest. Bridget fluttered away, landing atop the jars behind the counter.

A brute, heavy-browed and nearly the size of Tom, scowled in my face. The end of his club shoved me back until I stepped on Sally's foot. "Ow!" she said.

"*Que faites-vous ici?*" the brute growled.

"*Je suis chez moi,*" I said, startled.

A voice called weakly from upstairs. "*Qui est-ce, Henri?*"

"Simon?" I called back.

"Oh. *Laisse-les passer.*"

The brute grunted and lowered his club. We sidled

past him warily, then went upstairs to my bedroom.

Simon lay on his stomach, stripped naked. Dr. Kemp sat calmly on a chair he'd moved from one of the spare rooms, watching as his apprentice finished wrapping Simon in a fresh bandage. The doctor reached over to cover his patient in a bedsheet as Sally appeared, then grinned when he saw me rubbing my chest. "Charming fellow downstairs, eh?"

"Who . . . *what* . . . is that thing?" I said.

"Sorry," Simon said into his pillow, grimacing at the pain. "That's—ow!—Henri. My bodyguard. He's a bit overzealous, I admit—ungh! Must you make it so blasted tight?"

The apprentice looked to his master. Dr. Kemp rolled his eyes and motioned for the boy to continue. "You could have an infection instead, if you like."

"I loathe you, Doctor, as I do all your kind."

Dr. Kemp smirked. "As long as you pay the bill."

"I brought Henri with me when I came to England," Simon explained. "Found him in a tiny hamlet—argh!— near Calais. He was carrying a bale of hay, all by himself."

I believed it. "Where's the guard Lord Ashcombe left?"

"Gone with the marquess. Ashcombe stopped by this morning, and was good enough to send a man to the rooms

I've been renting to collect Henri. No offense to His Majesty, but I trust my own security better. Though the devil knows why someone would want to murder me."

"You're French," Dr. Kemp said. "That's reason enough."

"Can you see how many fingers I am holding up, Doctor?"

The physician laughed. "As you can see," he said to me, "the vicomte will be fine. I'll drop by each morning and night, and send Jack"—he indicated his apprentice—"to administer the poppy if you're not around. But just a few days more. I assume you know its dangers?"

I did. Though the poppy was unrivaled at fighting pain, it was extremely tricky to deal with. Give too much, and the patient would stop breathing. Give it too often, and the patient would become dependent on it, with terrible cravings. I assured Dr. Kemp we could move to willow bark extract whenever he ordered, and he and Jack left.

"Finally, some peace." Simon sounded drained. "I'm glad to see you again—Tom! Sally! You're well." Painfully, he held out a hand for the others to grasp. "What on earth happened to you all? Why weren't you in London?"

"Didn't you get my letters?" I said.

"What letters?"

I glanced over at Tom. "I sent you two while we were on the coast. One from Southampton, the other from Brighton, weeks ago."

"I received neither." Simon winced as he twisted, and Sally laid a hand on his shoulder for him to lie still. "That's why I'm in England. I sent you letters of my own, but never heard back. I was worried. So I decided to come and check on you.

"When I arrived, three weeks ago, I inquired at Whitehall, and was told you were off south with Ashcombe, though they wouldn't tell me why. I'd have gone to meet you, but they said you were already on your way back."

That had been the plan. We were supposed to have returned to Whitehall when the king did, in February, but another terrible storm kept us holed up in Brighton, irritating Lord Ashcombe to no end. "How did you know we'd arrived yesterday?"

"I was sent word the marquess had returned to the palace. I went there, but was told you hadn't come with him. I assumed you'd gone home. I'd just turned onto your street when I was attacked."

"By whom?" Sally said.

"I don't know. I didn't see them. I just stumbled, and felt a sharp pain in my back, and suddenly, I couldn't breathe. I thought I was about to faint."

"You were in shock," I said.

"Was that what it was? All I could think was: get to Blackthorn. Master Benedict will help. Stupid, isn't it? It's not like I didn't know he was gone."

I didn't think it was stupid. How many times had I called out, when I'd needed him?

"So you didn't see anybody?" Sally said. "Did the attacker say anything?"

"Ashcombe asked me the same question." Simon hesitated. "I told him no."

"That wasn't true?" I said.

"Well . . ."

"What was it?" Sally said.

"I must have I imagined it," Simon said, sounding embarrassed. "Or dreamed it, afterward, under the poppy. Because it doesn't make sense.

"I could have sworn I heard someone whisper, just before I was stabbed. They said . . . 'For the convent.'"

Tom's eyes went wide. "You were attacked by nuns?"

Simon made a face. "You see why I didn't want to mention it."

"You must have misheard them," Sally said.

"No doubt. But I don't know what else they could have said."

"Can you think of anyone who'd want to kill you?"

"Not in London," Simon said. "Not even in Paris, really, although you never know with those worms. But seriously, all my time in England, I lived in Nottinghamshire, not here. No one has any reason to murder me."

"The Raven does," I said slowly. "But you said he's dead."

"He is."

"How do you know?"

"Well, the Raven was Rémi, wasn't he?"

"I think so. Why?"

"Then he's definitely dead," Simon said, "because I saw Rémi's corpse."

CHAPTER

21

MY CHEST WAS TIGHT. "HOW DID you find him?"

"After you left," Simon said, "I spent a great many *livres* trying to track Rémi down. I contacted several old associates of Uncle Marin's, who were in the business of finding Templar artifacts for him. The information they provided was not always acquired . . . ethically. You understand my meaning?"

I nodded.

"I'd rather not have used them, but ordinary channels were getting me nowhere. Still, who better to catch a crook than a bunch of crooks themselves? You see, they'd heard of someone calling himself the Raven. By reputation, he was a man whose specialty was pretending to be someone else. He would infiltrate some noble's house, drain the coffers dry, and then disappear into the night—but not before murdering his former master.

"They claimed the Raven murdered people to reduce the chance of the victims coming for revenge. Can't chase after him if you're dead, yes? I suspect his motive was different." Simon's voice turned fierce. "I think he killed people just because he could. I think he *liked* it."

I thought very much the same.

"Anyway, he'd always got away with it before. I suppose he thought with Uncle Marin gone, and the estate's finances in shambles, I wouldn't be willing to go after him."

Simon's eyes burned. "He was wrong. I spent nearly every *sou* hunting him down. In the end, I should have stuck to my own kind. Because it wasn't the criminals who found him. It was another vicomte, Guy d'Auzon, living on an estate in the Val de Loire. I'd written to several landowners to be on the watch for Rémi, and possibly Colette—you remember her, the servant who fled with him?—applying for positions with false references. D'Auzon wrote back that they were there, and he'd already taken them in."

"What happened?" Tom said, breathless.

"I rode for the Val de Loire straight away. Unfortunately, the vicomte took matters into his own hands. He challenged them in his home, and they attacked. D'Auzon, rash but no fool, had already armed himself. He shot Rémi straight through the heart."

"What about Colette?" Sally said.

"Fled into the night, while the vicomte was reloading his pistol. Man should have brought two."

Suddenly I felt a lot better about wearing mine. I rested my hands on the grips.

"That's the way," Simon said wryly. "Anyway, by the time I got there, Rémi was already laid out on a bier in the cemetery. I examined the body myself. He'd grown a beard, and there was a fresh cut on his chin, but there was no doubt: It was him. And thus ends the Raven."

It was an amazing tale. And that should have been the end of it.

So why didn't I believe that it was over?

"We don't actually know," I said, "that Rémi was the Raven. We just assumed that."

Simon regarded me skeptically. "Who else could it have been?"

"A different man, behind Rémi, pulling the strings. For all we know, it could have been Colette."

"She was a pretty girl, Christopher, but not an intelligent one. Certainly not clever enough to be a criminal mastermind."

"Sounds like the perfect cover," I said. "Spread the word there's some man in charge of everything, then play the artless young maid."

Now everyone looked skeptical. "You're reaching," Simon said.

"I'm not. I'm just not jumping to conclusions. That's what I'm supposed to avoid, isn't it?"

"But you *are* jumping to conclusions," Simon said gently. "You saw the Raven as this larger-than-life figure, so you can't imagine him dead. In the end, all he was, was a man."

I stared out the window of my bedroom. "That's what everyone keeps telling me. But if the Raven's really gone, why were you attacked?"

"Maybe it wasn't to do with me at all," Simon said. "Maybe it's because of you. You and your king."

"What do you mean?"

"Ashcombe told me a girl was murdered yesterday at the palace. I was there, Christopher—very likely there when it happened. He also suggested you're in service to the king now, though he didn't say exactly how. So: A murder happens in Whitehall. You're part of the investigation. I've made no secret of why I'm in London, and no secret that I was coming to see you. Whether it was mistaken identity, or eliminating one of your allies, I suspect whoever attacked me is wrapped up in whatever it is you're doing. And that's nothing to do with the Raven. Is it?"

No. As far as I could tell, it wasn't.

I still didn't accept that Rémi was necessarily the Raven. Colette was a ridiculous suspect, true. But all we really knew was that Master Benedict had been, according to the letter the Raven had sent me in France, a thorn in his side for a long time.

I stopped.

Thinking of Master Benedict made me think of Paris. Not of the Raven. Of the clues we'd followed to solve the riddles.

And now I couldn't get that thought out of my mind.

"Maybe you're right," I said. "Are you in much pain?"

Simon looked at me askance. "Is my constant grimace not enough of a hint?"

I gave him an embarrassed grin. "Sorry. I'll prepare the poppy."

I set water to boil down in the workshop. Bridget joined me, trying to poke her beak into the cork that stopped the jars. Once the pot was over the fire, I asked Tom and Sally to help me look for Master Benedict's coding device. "It's in one of the spare rooms. I can't remember which."

"What does it look like?" Sally said.

I described it to them. "Everyone take a different room. What?"

Tom watched me with narrowed eyes. "You're up to something."

Was I that easy to read? I beckoned them close, so Henri, in the shop, couldn't hear. I wasn't sure if he knew English, but I wasn't going to take any chances.

"This whole business," I said, "with the letters I've been getting, and the codes. Does it feel familiar to you?"

"You mean running around the city," Tom said, "chasing clues that will almost certainly get us killed? I thought that's just what we did now."

"I'm serious."

"So am I."

"A letter appears in my home," I said, "with no apparent way of it getting there. It holds a riddle, and a cipher—that leads us to *another* riddle, and *another* cipher. And I bet, once we've solved the second one, it will send us off to hunt down a third. Doesn't that feel like something we've done before?"

Sally frowned. "Paris," she said. "It feels like what we did in Paris."

"And who was making us run around in Paris?"

It dawned on them at the same time. They stared at me. "You mean . . . ," Tom began.

I nodded, leaned in, and whispered, "I'm pretty sure I know who's sending me these letters. It's the Templars."

CHAPTER
22

"TEMPLARS?" TOM SAID, AMAZED.
"In London?"

"Why not?" I said. "Their order was everywhere before it was disbanded. Why wouldn't they be here, too?"

"I'd believe it," Sally said. "But if it's the Templars, and they're trying to help us, why bother with all the riddles? It's not like we don't know they still exist. Why don't they just tell you what they want you to do?"

That's what I didn't understand. Though Tom had an idea.

"What if it's a test?" Suddenly he gasped. "They're testing us for entry into the order!"

"You mean . . . they want us to join the Templars?" I said.

"Yes! In Paris, Father Bernard said they needed to get new knights from somewhere."

"He also said we needed to be older."

"We *are* older."

"I'm pretty sure he meant years, not months."

Still, it wasn't the craziest idea. If the puzzles were being sent by the Templars—and it really felt like they were—what other reason would they have for being so obscure? The thought made my blood race a little faster. And scared me a little, too.

I needed to think about it. "Let's find Master Benedict's coding device."

Searching gave me plenty of time to mull it over. Master Benedict had kept a tidy shop, but a cluttered house. Part of that was the ever-growing hoard of books he was forever buying, but there were all sorts of curios, gewgaws, and devices that sparked his interest, too. Once I'd given Simon the poppy, it took us the better part of an hour to find what we were looking for, inside a sack at the bottom of a box of old clothes.

I took the sack and collected the others, including

Bridget. Simon, under the poppy's effect, had already fallen asleep. I left a small pot of the infusion with Henri, and told him he could give the medicine to Simon again only after another six hours had passed. I hoped he'd remember. All he did was grunt.

Tom was confused as to why we were leaving Blackthorn. "I thought you wanted to solve the puzzle."

"I do," I said. "Just not here."

Sally glanced over at Henri, who was picking his teeth behind the shop counter. "Are you worried . . . ?"

"No, nothing like that." I led them outside, where we huddled in the street near our horses. "I know you're convinced the Raven's gone, but I'm not. I want to be sure. He claimed he'd known Master Benedict. So let's see if we can find more about that. And let's see what we can discover about the Templars, too."

"Where on earth are we going to learn about Templars?" Tom asked.

"If you want to find secrets," I said, "where better than a secret library?"

CHAPTER 23

THE BOOKSHOP WAS TUCKED AWAY

in the darker part of Saint Bennet's Hill, a street near the
Thames, just south of Saint Paul's Cathedral. The shop had
no storefront and no windows to look through. There was
only a single iron-banded door, squeezed between shipping
warehouses. Nailed to the door was a plate, announcing
what was inside.

RARE TOMES

PROPRIETOR, ISAAC CHANDLER

ALL WHO SEEK KNOWLEDGE ARE WELCOME

Above it, carved into the stone, was a phrase in Latin: FIAT LUX. Let there be light.

I thumped on the door. Isaac, an old friend of Master Benedict's, had become a friend of mine after my master's murder. But I was afraid.

The last time I'd seen him had been during the plague. To ensure his own safety, and more important, the safety of the secret alchemy library beneath his shop, he'd quarantined himself down there, with no plans to return to the surface for six months.

That's what had me scared. I wasn't worried about Isaac's supplies; he'd stocked up on plenty of food, and even had a well for water and a pit for waste in the hideout below. I was afraid because when I'd seen him last, he hadn't looked so good.

He was older than Master Benedict, well into his seventies. Underground living would have been hard on him. I thumped again, to no response.

"What do we do?" Tom said, worried now, too. "Break the door down?"

The thing was oak. The iron bands wouldn't help. We'd need a battering ram to crack it.

I stepped back, looked up. There was a chimney in the building; smoke was coming out of it. I couldn't tell if that came from Isaac's home, or was part of the neighboring warehouses. "Maybe we can find a place to climb up—"

"Shh!" Sally said. She had her head to the door, listening. "I hear something."

It was hard to imagine anything could be heard through *that* door. But then came the clack of a lock, and another, and the door swung open.

It was Isaac. My heart leaped at the sight of him, even as I noticed he looked terrible. His face was haggard, dark circles under his eyes. He'd lost more of his wispy white hair, and he stood hunched, as if mere standing was just about too much for him.

His eyes, a little cloudy, peered out. He adjusted his spectacles and saw Sally first.

"Yes, my dear?" he began.

And then he saw me and Tom.

He slumped in relief, and some of his years melted away. He reached for us, took our hands, and held them. "Boys," he said, voice thick. "I had feared . . ."

We hugged him, and it felt like coming home.

. . .

Isaac could hardly believe he was seeing us again. "When I ended my quarantine," he said, "I sent a courier to Blackthorn. He told me it had been abandoned. So I sent him to Tom's house, and he saw the cross, and . . . I thought . . ."

I'd forgotten about that. The red cross of the plague had been painted on Tom's door. With his family still on the boat, no one had returned to remove it.

"We were spared," I said. "You didn't find us because we weren't in London."

He was surprised at that. "Where did you go?"

"We should talk inside," I said. "It's quite a story."

With the front door locked again, I introduced him to Sally. "She's one of us," I said, and he caught my meaning: We had no secrets.

Isaac took us upstairs, to his quarters above the shop. Although he seemed rejuvenated by our return, he moved awfully slowly up the steps. Delicately, like a man in constant pain.

As they were too narrow for either Tom or me to walk beside him, Sally lent him an arm, which he patted gratefully. He leaned on her all the way up.

His quarters were simple, just a kitchen and a bedroom.

The real space was deep below the shop, in the secret library, which had once been a Templar sanctuary, centuries ago. Isaac put on a pot of coffee to brew.

"How I missed this," he said wistfully as the aroma of roasted beans filled the room. "Quarantine living, as you might imagine, has very few charms."

He listened, then, as I told him everything that had happened since he'd gone underground—and I did tell him everything, because Isaac and I had no secrets, either. He was saddened to hear of Dr. Parrett's death, even more of Marin Chastellain's. But he was delighted about our pensions and intrigued by my new position as apprentice spymaster.

"Benedict would have approved," he said.

"You really think so?"

"You know his penchant for secrets. He was never a spy's apprentice, of course, but his skill with codes was widely known. He even worked, for a time, with the spymaster of Charles I, when he was younger. The man sent him ciphers, and he'd send them back solved, if he could. He stopped with the coming of the Commonwealth; he disliked how they treated our previous king. But he started up again once Charles took back his throne. He might even have corresponded with your new master—what's his name again?"

"Lord Walsingham."

"Yes, that's him."

I was surprised the spymaster hadn't mentioned it.

"So," Isaac continued, "you learn more about codes, but still get to be an apothecary in the end? His Majesty has looked after you quite well, I think."

His words made me feel so much better. *Is this really all right?* I asked my master, and I thought I could see him smile.

That weight a little lighter, I finished the story. And, there really being no secrets between us, I told him what I'd told no one else, not even Lord Ashcombe.

I told him about the Templars.

"Incredible," Isaac said.

I showed him the Templar florin, the gold coin the Templars had given me as a token of their gratitude for my helping them in Paris. He turned it over, marveling at it.

"Rumors of their existence have lingered for centuries," he said, awed. "I believed them—our little society of alchemists has lived for generations, why not the Knights Templar?—but I never imagined I'd see proof."

"That's part of why we came here," I said. "I think the

Templars are the ones sending me these riddles. I was wondering if there was anything more you could tell me about them."

He studied the two letters I'd received. Then he stared into his coffee, watching the steam rise, thinking.

"There isn't much," he said. "Most of the writing on the Templars is about their history. What remains is largely conjecture."

He frowned. "Though there is this one document. It's a statement, taken during an interrogation, some thirty, forty years ago? I can't remember if Charles I was king, or James. Either way, the man claimed to be a Templar. He gave a decent account of their order. Assuming he's to be believed."

"Do you know where it is?" I said, excited.

"In the library, underground. It won't be hard to find. What concerns me more is this business about the Raven."

"That was the other reason we came." I showed him the letter the Raven had sent to Maison Chastellain in Paris.

My dear Christopher,

I congratulate you on your victory. You have done the impossible: You found the Templar treasure, where others—including me—could not. Don't worry, I'll tell no one the truth of what happened; I like that you and I now share a secret. And, as vexed as I am, I must admit: It was fascinating to watch your mind at work. I see now why Master Benedict chose you as an apprentice.

Does the mention of your master surprise you? No doubt Blackthorn never told you about me, so I will: He was a thorn in my side for many years. Now, though he has departed, you come to take his place. And while I try not to begrudge you your success, your discovery has cost me dearly. You owe me, Christopher. And I always collect what I am owed.

Your first payment is the life of Marin Chastellain. No, he did not die from his illness. I poisoned him—and in doing so, I left you a clue. Before you go searching for it, I want you to know that I did not kill him because he was any threat to me. I did it because I knew it would hurt Blackthorn, and, in turn, hurt you. It is, after all, much more sporting to face an opponent who understands the stakes of the game.

I am going to do to you what I should have done to

Blackthorn years ago: I am going to make you suffer. I will do this by taking away the things you love, one by one, until there is only you and me. And then, once I have stripped your life bare, you will understand.

Find the clue I've left for you. Ponder it. Then reflect on what it might mean. There's no need to rush; I have several plans in motion that must be completed before our game can truly begin. So, until then, be well, Christopher. Savor your life, while you still have some of it left. For when I am ready, I will come for you.

The Raven

Isaac read it, disturbed. "What was the clue the Raven left?" he asked.

"I think it was a pigeon feather," I said. "We found it tucked under Marin's mattress. It had to have been placed there deliberately."

"Do you know what it means?"

"I was hoping you would."

He shook his head. "Benedict always kept pigeons, as you well know." He nodded toward Bridget. "Beyond that? Nothing comes to mind."

I told him we'd thought that Rémi was the Raven and described him. "Simon said he's dead. But in the letter, the Raven claims Master Benedict was his enemy. Can you think of who that might be?"

Isaac mulled it over. "Hard to say. I don't recognize Rémi's description, but the man might have met Benedict years ago, so he wouldn't look like he did last November. What's more, he could have met him during his travels, maybe in France. I doubt I've ever seen him." He regarded me. "You're not certain this Rémi was the Raven, then?"

"I just want to make sure."

"Understandable. Unfortunately, your description narrows down nothing. Your master made countless enemies over the years, some quite serious."

"He did?"

Isaac smiled. "You loved Benedict, so you're forgetting how abrasive he could be with those he thought ridiculous. He had many, many arguments with other apothecaries, physicians, even Parliament, about all sorts of things. The proper preparation of remedies, the care of patients, the management of outbreaks . . . Half of his opponents he thought quacks; the others, fools, and he was never shy about stating it. Being well respected—if not always well liked—meant he ruined many a reputation over the years. In London *and* abroad."

"So we'll never really know," I said, disappointed.

"Not necessarily. Benedict kept detailed journals, all the way back to his own days as an apprentice. He'll certainly have noted his nastier opponents—and it's the pure viciousness in this letter that worries me. Perhaps we might find something there."

I'd read some of Master Benedict's journals before. One had even been a great help during the plague. "I have a few at home."

Isaac nodded. "Benedict stored the rest downstairs, so I'll have any years you're missing. If you bring what you have to me, I'll go through them in detail. See if anything sparks my memory."

"We should work out this new message first," Sally said.

Everyone agreed that was more pressing. Isaac studied the second letter, reading the line before the puzzle. "*La ruota dell'italiano,*" he said. "You understand what it's asking?"

"I have the device here," I said, holding up the sack I'd brought from Blackthorn. "I can solve the code. It's the riddles I don't really understand. Not even the first one."

I spread the letters out, and we looked at the first rhyming couplet.

An oath was made, a promise sworn,
To those who wished to bind him.

But he returned, and offered scorn,
And so they come to find him.

"Lord Walsingham thought that was a threat against the king," I said.

"I would tend to agree," Isaac said, "and not just because of the murders at Whitehall. Charles is well known for breaking oaths."

"He is?" Tom said, disappointed.

"Indeed. He's a generous ruler, as you've all discovered, but a slippery one, when he wishes to be. Many a time he's made a promise, then broken it when it was not to his advantage. Which does, unfortunately, make it difficult to decide who this current enemy is. Have you found any more clues?"

"Well . . ." I looked at the others. "When Simon was attacked, he thought he heard the assassin say something."

"What was it?"

"'For the convent.'"

Isaac looked at me over his spectacles, amused. "No doubt Simon misheard. But that would mean the true curse was something close. Convent . . . con . . . vent . . ."

"Covent, maybe?" Sally said.

"Like Covent Garden?" I said. "That's just north of the palace."

"The market?" Tom said. "Our enemies aren't nuns—they're fruits?"

Isaac smiled. "Also unlikely. But this may be the right track. Convent . . . Covent . . . oh."

He sat up, eyes alight.

"Yes," he said. "I know what this riddle means."

CHAPTER

24

"WHAT IS IT?" I SAID.

Isaac sipped his coffee. "What do you know of the Civil Wars? Before His Majesty was sent into exile, I mean."

"Just what I learned in Cripplegate." For Master Benedict, the Civil Wars fell under the realm of politics, so he'd ignored them in my education. "Oliver Cromwell led the troops of Parliament to overthrow the previous king, Charles I. Our current king, Charles II, went to Scotland after his father was executed. Cromwell then came for him, Parliament's troops won, and His Majesty had to flee into exile for good."

"A fair summary," Isaac said, "if lacking in certain

details. The key points you miss concern our current king.

"Charles was in France when his father was executed. England, then, under the control of Oliver Cromwell and the Commonwealth, abolished the monarchy. But our king is king of England *and* Scotland, and the Scots were *not* willing to give up the throne. In fact, they were quite angry that Cromwell had executed Charles I, as he was their king, too, and they'd been assured of his safety.

"So the Scots suggested that Charles II rule from the north. However, they refused to let him into the country unless he signed an oath.

"The wars, you see, had become religious. The English were ruled by Puritans under Cromwell, while the Scots were Presbyterian. And the Puritans did much to try and stamp out every faith but their own.

"Scotland wanted not only to defend its own religion, but to spread it to England. So the Scots forced Charles II to sign a treaty accepting a document that promised to spread Presbyterianism, and stamp out other religions. The document was named the Solemn League and *Covenant*."

I sat up. "Covenant. That's what Simon heard. Not 'for the convent.' *For the Covenant*."

"But this treaty was signed, what, fifteen years ago?"

Sally said. "Why are they coming for His Majesty now?"

"That's where the rest of the history matters," Isaac said. "The treaty was a humiliation for Charles. He hated the Covenant, yet not only was he forced to sign it, he was then made to sit through constant lectures about the evils of his ways, and of his father in particular. By the time Cromwell came for him, Charles loathed not only the Covenant, but all of Scotland as well.

"When the Commonwealth finally fell in 1660, and Charles returned to his throne, the Scots expected our king to honor the Covenant. Instead, His Majesty rejected it, and took revenge on those who'd humiliated him. That might have ended things, but Charles appointed governors over Scotland who hate its people as much as he does.

"As you might imagine, this has not gone well. There's been unrest up north for years. I promise you, open rebellion is coming. I'm surprised we haven't seen it already."

"So the threats against the king . . . ," Tom began.

"Are almost certainly from Covenanters," Isaac finished. "They'd gladly assassinate him if they could."

I thought of the Scotsmen who'd been waiting outside the palace gates. *Another English slight!* one had said, outraged. And the other . . . he'd followed us into the Banqueting House.

Were they part of the threat?

I had no way of knowing. And there was something about all this that didn't add up. "If it's Covenanters," I said, "and they're after the king, why murder the servant girls? Simon, I can just understand—if they think I'm going to help His Majesty, and Simon is with me . . . but why a pair of maids? It doesn't make sense."

"To kill a king," Isaac said, "you have to get close to him. Charles spends his days inside Whitehall, surrounded by armed guards. They can't just raise an army to attack the palace."

"But if they *infiltrated* the palace, put an assassin inside—"

"And if the servants spotted something wrong!" Sally said. "Servants see everything. They'd need to be silenced."

It all fit. The threat against the king, the riddle's broken oath, the maids murdered at Whitehall. I thought again of the Scotsmen at the gate—and wondered if this was what Walsingham thought, too. I'd have to tell him what we'd discovered.

"So," I said. "Covenanters are trying to kill the king. And the Templars are trying to help us stop them."

"I still don't see why we have to go through all these riddles," Tom said.

Isaac placed the second puzzle on the table. "Let's try solving it and find out."

We all huddled over the letter.

Saints defend these ancient walls,
Saints we hope will save,

Visit them in hallowed halls,
And pray upon his grave.

la ruota dell'italiano

B s m v & h c t c q q t d k d & l x

"'Saints defend these ancient walls,'" Tom repeated. "Which walls? London's?"

"Or someplace in London," I said. "Whitehall, maybe? If the king is under threat?"

"'Saints we hope will save,'" Sally quoted. "Does that mean . . . patron saints?"

Isaac nodded. "That would fit the riddle. If it is patron saints, then I'd guess 'ancient walls' refers to the city. London has several."

"Saint Paul," Tom said.

"Michael as well. Though he's an archangel, not a saint."

"There's another *M* name," I said. "Master Benedict showed me a book of them once. Mel-something . . . Mellitus?"

"Who's that?" Sally said.

"First bishop of London, I think."

Tom was frowning. "There's another, too. Something to do with a pilgrimage. I can't remember his name. It sounded funny. Like Erwin, or something."

We all looked at one another, but no one knew.

"Solve the code," Isaac suggested. "That may make the riddle clear."

"You keep saying you know how," Tom said to me. "Are you going to show us or not?"

"Sure," I said. "The secret is this line, here: '*la ruota dell'italiano.*' It means 'the Italian's wheel.'"

I opened the sack I'd taken from Blackthorn and pulled out the device inside.

CHAPTER
25

"THIS IS IT," I SAID. "THE ITALIAN'S

wheel is *Alberti's disk.*"

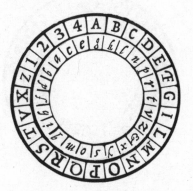

"What is that thing?" Tom said.

"A decoding device. Two wheels, made of wood, joined in the center. Both have an alphabet on them. The outer disk is fixed in place, but the inner disk can move."

I flicked the smaller wheel inside. It spun around a couple of times before coming to a stop.

"It's basically a substitution cipher, like a simple letter shift. With Alberti's disk, you match the *coded* letters on the *inside* wheel, to the *true* letters on the *outside* wheel. The solution depends on how the wheels are aligned. Change them by even one place"—I moved the inner disk—"and you get a totally different substitution."

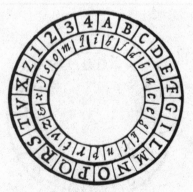

"That's what makes Alberti's disk so clever," I said. "It changes position all the time."

Sally leaned in, curious. "How do you know where to set the wheels?"

"There are two ways to do it," I said. "The first is by using a key, like with Vigenère. But we haven't been given a key. Instead, the first letter of the cipher is a capital letter. See?"

B s m v & h c t c q q t d k d & l x

"The *B* refers to the letter *B* on the outer disk. That tells you to align the *B* with the *index* letter on the inner disk. Alberti usually chose the letter *k* as the index. So we begin by aligning the *B* on the outside with the *k* on the inside."

I moved the wheels so they were properly aligned.

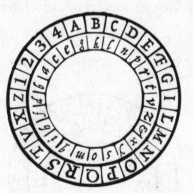

"Now we decipher the message. *s* is matched with *P*, so the first letter in the message is *P*."

Bridget marched across the paper as I wrote the letter down.

B s m v & h c t c q q t d k d & l x
P

"Next, *m* matches with *R*. And so on. *v* becomes *I*. Ampersand becomes *M*. *h* becomes *V*. *c* becomes . . . oh, it's a *3*."

B s m v & h c t c q q t d k d & l x
P R I M V 3

"What does that mean?" Tom said.

"A number tells us it's time to move the disk," I said. "And also how. First we scratch out the *3* from our message. Then we move the inner disk so the letter that gave us the number—in this case, *c*—is now under the *A*."

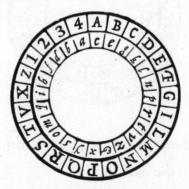

B s m v & h c t c q q t d k d & l x
P R I M V 3

"There," I said. "Now we have a whole new substitution. And we continue as before. *t* becomes *L*, *c* is now *A*, *q* is *V* . . ."

I continued, filling in the message, until I got a 2.

B s m v & h c t c q q t d k d & l x
P R I M V 3 L A V V L 2

"Another number," I said. "So we shift the inner disk again, so the *d* that got us the *2* is under the *A*."

"Throw out the *2*, and continue. *k* becomes *G* . . . and so on . . . until we're finished."

B s m v & h c t c q q t d k d & l x

P R I M V 3 L A V V L 2 G A R I S

"Now we write it out without the numbers, and we get . . ."

P R I M V L A V V L G A R I S

"It didn't work," Sally said.

"Yes, it did," I said. "The message is clear. It's just not in *English.*"

CHAPTER

26

"WHAT IS IT, THEN?" TOM SAID.

Isaac understood. "It's Latin. The Latin alphabet only has twenty-three letters. There's no *J*, *U*, or *W*. That's why there are so many *V*s in the message. Some are actually *U*. Write it out," he told me.

I did as he said.

PRIMVLA   VVLGARIS
primula   vulgaris

"I still don't know what that is," Tom said.

"Primrose," I said. "*Primula vulgaris* is the apothecary name for common primrose."

"The flower?" Sally said. "How does that help us?"

"Perhaps," Isaac said, "it goes with the riddle."

Saints defend these ancient walls,
Saints we hope will save,

Visit them in hallowed halls,
And pray upon his grave.

"Pray upon his grave," Sally said. "Oh. So you would . . . put flowers there? Primroses?"

"Or maybe the primroses are already there," I said, "and we're supposed to find them."

"All right, so where's 'his' grave? Where are the hallowed halls?"

"Something to do with the saints, I guess."

Suddenly Tom gasped.

"I know." He sprang from his chair, sending Bridget flapping away to safety. "I know! I *know*!"

"Where is it?" Sally said.

"Erkenwald!"

She looked confused. "Where?"

"Not where. *Who.* Saint Erkenwald. He's a patron saint of London. Reverend Wright talked about him at service last year. Or maybe two years ago. When he was telling us how we should make a pilgrimage. Do you remember?"

"Er . . ." I didn't recall this at all. But then my mind usually drifted during Reverend Wright's sermons.

"He told us about Saint Erkenwald," Tom insisted, "and about how people would make pilgrimages to London to visit his tomb."

"But where *is* his tomb?" Sally said.

"In the 'hallowed halls' of Saint Paul's Cathedral! Do you see? It fits. Visit *them*—the saints, Paul and Erkenwald—in the cathedral, and pray upon *his* grave. That's Erkenwald's tomb!"

That made perfect sense. I looked up at him, amazed.

"I got it! I got it!" Tom marched around the room. "Look at me, I'm a spy, too." He hid behind the doorjamb, peeking his head out.

Sally giggled.

"Told you the hat makes me smarter," he said.

"I suppose it does," I said, trying not to laugh. "We'll go to Saint Paul's, then. But leave the hat behind for this one."

He clutched it to his chest. "What? Why?"

"Because if we're going to another letter drop, I want to be quiet about it. And that hat . . . isn't."

Disappointed, Tom left it on Isaac's table, commiserating with Sally. "He just doesn't understand fashion."

"I know," she said sympathetically. I couldn't tell if she was humoring him, or whether I should actually be offended.

We hurried away, getting halfway down the steps before remembering Isaac wouldn't be hurrying anywhere. He leaned on Sally to help him navigate the stairs again, going even more slowly down than up.

"Take this." Isaac reached under his shirt and removed his key, hanging from a string around his neck. He shuffled toward the back of his counter, and, with some effort, pulled on the book that cracked the bookcase open, leading to the secret library downstairs.

Sally lingered, watching him. As I unlocked the front door, she put a hand on my arm, speaking quietly. "I'm going to stay."

"You are? Why?"

"How many stairs did you say it was down to the library?"

I looked over at Isaac. With difficulty, he heaved the bookcase open.

Too many, I thought.

"He needs help, Christopher," Sally said. "I can help. I want to."

"We'll all stay," Tom said.

Sally shook her head. "Christopher has to finish this puzzle. And you have to be there in case anything goes wrong. Give me Bridget. I'll stay here and search the library, find out what Isaac has about the Templars. It'll be faster for everyone."

She had said she wanted to be useful. "All right," I said, handing her my pigeon. "Saint Paul's is just up the street. We'll hurry back."

"Be careful."

We assured her we would be, but really, we were going to a church.

What could go wrong?

CHAPTER

27

IT WAS SUPPOSED TO BE IMPRESSIVE.

Saint Paul's Cathedral was the heart of the Church for London's faithful and had been for four hundred years. Over five hundred feet long, it should have stood as a shining beacon in a troubled city.

But the place looked awful. The spire, once the tallest in Christendom, had collapsed in a fire long before I was born and had never been replaced. The buttressed arches sagged, the stone walls cracking underneath. The stained glass, once beautiful, was dull and filthy.

To say nothing of the souls of those around it. The outer grounds of the cathedral had become an open-air market for Protestant booksellers and doomsday preachers. A man on a box screamed at us about the end times as we passed. A second, standing beside him in a ragged robe and bare feet, hollered about the Day of Judgment, trying—and failing—to drown out his opponent.

It wasn't much better inside. The long stretch of the nave, called Paul's Walk, had become something of a market, too, with merchants of all kinds doing business between the giant pillars that rose to the arched roof high above us. Others hung about, trading in the latest gossip of the city.

I shook my head. The last time I'd been here, I'd thought Saint Paul's something special. But after seeing Notre-Dame in Paris, I found myself ashamed of this place. Tom, devout and full of English pride, seemed particularly embarrassed, and even a little cross. He muttered under his breath at the merchants; the ones who caught the look in his eyes found somewhere else to be.

Well, we weren't here for worship, anyway. I found a boy sweeping the mud tracked in by visitors and asked him for Saint Erkenwald's tomb.

"Round the chancel, my lord," he said. "Directly behind the altar."

We went up one dais, then another, into the chancel. Here were the first people we saw actually praying, or visiting the shrines, monuments, and tombs of those interred in the church. Past the chancel, on the eastern side, were three chapels, dedicated to Mary, Saint George, and Saint Dunstan. Hallowed halls, indeed.

Tom pointed. "There it is." Right up against the divider that separated the chapels from the chancel was Saint Erkenwald's resting place.

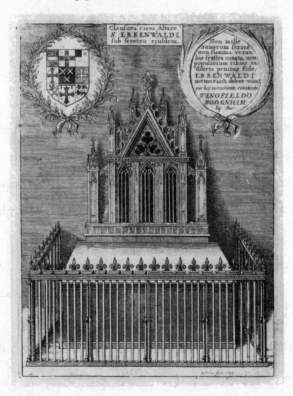

His tomb was a long, flat-topped burial vault. Behind it, against the divider, was a carved stone image of the side of some cathedral, all pillars, arches, and windows. The area was fenced off by a wrought-iron rail, topped with iron fleurs-de-lis. The rail was low enough that pilgrims could place offerings on the tomb. There were a few already: a pouch, knotted with rope; a silver shilling; a seashell, polished to gleaming.

And there was something else, too.

"Look."

Next to the shilling was a bunch of pale yellow, five-petaled flowers. Their long, slender stems were tied together with string.

"Those are primroses," I said.

Tom was proud his guess had turned out to be correct. "What now?"

The riddle said *pray upon his grave.* Were we meant to take that literally?

There were several people praying there already. I moved closer, trying not to make it obvious I was looking them over. As far as I could tell, they seemed to be ordinary pilgrims. As for the primroses—

There.

I nudged Tom. Deep among the pale yellow flowers, someone had tucked a paper, folded tight. "That must be what we're looking for," I whispered, and I stepped toward the rail.

Tom yanked me back by my collar.

"What do you think you're doing?" he said.

"Taking the primroses," I said, puzzled.

"You can't steal flowers from Saint Erkenwald."

"I'm not. Those flowers were meant for us. Look, there's a note and everything—"

He yanked me back again.

"I let you get away with a lot of things," Tom said. "I even let you steal a painting from the Louvre—"

"We *swapped* a painting from the Louvre," I protested.

"—but I am not letting you rob a saint!"

"I told you: It's not robbing if it's meant for us. Look, I'll just grab the note—will you please let go?"

Tom kept his fingers wrapped firmly around my collar. "And what do you imagine will happen," he said, "when everyone sees you take something from the grave?"

That was a fair point. There were plenty of faithful around. If they saw me reach over and grab the flowers, they might think I was a thief. I'd end up with a good thumping—if I was lucky.

"So what am I supposed to do?" I said.

Tom didn't have an answer for that. "I suppose we could wait until no one's watching."

"With this crowd? We could be here till midnight. What we need is a distraction."

"Oh no," Tom said.

I snapped my fingers. "That's it."

"Oh *no*."

"Fireworks!" I said. "I still have two of them in my sash."

Tom stared at me. "You want to shoot fireworks . . . at Saint Erkenwald?"

"Not *at*—how little you think of me," I said, genuinely offended.

"It's not like I don't have good reason."

"Name *one time* I set fire to a saint."

"You burned down the king's carriage!"

"That's not a saint! And it was an *accident*! Are you ever going to let that go?"

"Let it go? It happened yesterday!"

"Always stuck in the past, you are."

"You're the one talking about fireworks!"

"*Outside,*" I said. "I was going to say we shoot them *outside.*"

That mollified Tom a bit. Still, he said, "What would that do? No one will see them in the cathedral. Were you going to announce it? 'Hey, everyone, stop praying and come see the show?'"

He was irritating me—even more so because he had a point. "Fine. Let me think of something else."

"I'm just saying the answer doesn't always have to be fire."

I glared at him before turning back to the pilgrims. I couldn't think of anything that would draw their attention away from the tomb—at least nothing Tom would let me do.

If I couldn't distract them, then I'd need some way of getting to the vault without them noticing what I was doing. Some of the pilgrims had left offerings. Maybe if I did the same?

I stared at the primroses on the tomb. "That's it," I said.

"What is?"

"I have an idea."

"Oh *no,*" Tom said.

I stormed out of the church.

CHAPTER

28

I STOPPED AT THE ENTRANCE, looking around.

"Where are you going?" Tom said.

"I'm looking for . . . there. Come on."

We hurried past the preachers to the edge of the cathedral grounds, where booksellers touted their wares to passersby. Beside them, huddled in worn clothes, was a girl of about ten. A quartet of baskets lay at her feet, full of flowers.

"Cooee!" she called. "Flowers, o! Flowers, o! Flowers!" As she saw Tom and me approach, her face, thin and gaunt, turned hopeful. "Flowers, my lord? Handpicked."

I scanned her baskets for pale yellow. Sure enough, she

had a few primroses. "Did anyone buy some of those today?"

"No one, my lord." She sounded resigned. "It's hard going, even with the sickness gone. Haven't sold anything for three days now."

The girl's hands were red from the chill, her fingers scarred with the pricks of thorns. The deep winter had taken its toll on her. If she weighed three-quarters as much as Sally, I'd have been surprised.

"How much?" I said.

She brightened. "A farthing a bunch. Picked them fresh myself, honest."

"No, sorry, I meant how much for the lot?"

Her eyes went wide. "All of them?" She cast a quick glance over her baskets. "Sixpence?"

I reached into the coin purse Lord Ashcombe had given me and handed her six pennies. She stared, like she couldn't quite tell if she was dreaming. "Thank you, my lord, thank you."

The girl and I began to load the flowers into Tom's arms, until I could barely see his face.

He sneezed. "Why do *I* have to carry these?"

"Because you wouldn't let me use the fireworks," I said.

I stuffed the final bunch under Tom's collar. The flower

seller tugged on my sleeve. "I'm here every day, my lord. Or," she said desperately, "if you like, I can bring flowers fresh to your home? New flowers every morn, wouldn't that be lovely?"

I didn't really have any need for flowers. But I felt terrible for the girl. Here she was, scrounging every freezing morning in the meadows, hoping to earn a farthing, when I'd just got a pension from the king. And all because Master Benedict had taken me in, three and a half years ago.

"You think Sally would like some flowers?" I asked Tom.

He nudged the petals aside with his chin and grinned. "I *bet* she would."

"You're just going to keep saying that, aren't you?"

"For the rest of my life." He sneezed. "Which, at this rate, may not be all that long."

I handed the girl a half crown—worth two shillings and sixpence, or the equivalent of thirty pennies. "Bring flowers for a week," I said, "to Berkshire House, on Saint James's Park. Say they're for Sally Deschamps."

She pinched the silver, barely able to believe it was real. Then she hid it away safe in her dress. "Every day, my lord. I promise, no matter what, you'll see. I'll bring the best for your sweetheart."

Tom made a strangled noise.

I flushed. "She's *not* my sweetheart."

The girl gave me a knowing smile. "As you like, my lord."

Tom couldn't hold it in any longer. He laughed. Then he sneezed. Then he laughed again.

Everyone's against me.

At least Tom was in a better mood.

"So what are we going to do with all these—*atchoo!*" Back in the church, people paused to watch the sniffling giant carrying flowers through the nave. "Give them to the pilgrims and sneeze them to death?"

"I don't think that's a verb," I said. "Well . . . it is a verb, but I don't think you can use it that way."

"I don't need a grammar lesson. I need a handkerchief."

"We'll be rid of them in a second. Pardon me, sir."

We'd reached the pilgrims praying at Saint Erkenwald's tomb. They parted, allowing the two of us through to the rail. I began placing the flowers all over the vault.

"In memory of our mother," I said to a woman looking puzzled. "Let me just make some space."

I pushed the offerings farther toward the center of the

tomb. As the flowers piled up, they blocked everyone's view of what was already on the stone. Tom, finally realizing what I was doing, stood in front of the pilgrims to help cover me. When no one could see, I reached into the primroses and palmed the note, slipping it into my doublet.

We stepped back through the crowd. Tom blew his nose, a honk that echoed in the rafters. "That was clever," he said.

I was feeling somewhat proud myself. I pulled the note from my pocket and began to unfold it when suddenly a cry came from behind us.

"Hey! What are you doing? Stop!"

Tom and I whirled. The man who'd shouted was a priest in a cassock, standing near the chapel to Saint Dunstan. I covered my doublet where I'd stuffed the note, feeling— and no doubt looking—absurdly guilty.

But the priest wasn't shouting at us. He'd stretched out his hand to someone else nearby. This man was dressed in a tight doublet and coat, with a cape and a wide-brimmed hat. His lower face was black, and for one ridiculous moment, I thought he was sporting an absurdly large beard.

Then I realized he was wearing a scarf. The man had pulled it up, covering his nose, concealing everything but his eyes.

And in his hand he held a long, slim dagger.

CHAPTER

I STARED AT THE DAGGER, STUNNED.

But . . . this is a church, I thought stupidly.

The man stared back. His eyes were cold and empty, the soul of a killer. Still I didn't understand.

Why?

I had no more time to think. Tom grabbed my collar and yanked me backward—this time, not quite so gently. He literally threw me behind him, sending me tumbling through the pilgrims to sprawl on the floor. The back of my skull hit the railing around Saint Erkenwald's tomb. The iron—and my head—rang like a bell.

I barely felt it. As the pilgrims scattered, I had a clear

line of sight to the assassin. He advanced toward me.

Then Tom stepped in the way.

He reached over his shoulder and pulled the cloth from his sword, his right hand on Eternity's hilt. He drew the weapon upward, but barely, just an inch, so the forte of the blade glinted, gold letters pressed into shining steel. He held his left hand out toward the assassin, in imitation of the priest, but this gesture was a threat. *Don't come any closer.*

I didn't understand why Tom hadn't drawn his blade. Then I realized it was for the same reason my own brain had taken so long to work in the first place. *This is a church.*

The assassin sidestepped, left and right, trying to catch sight of me again. Tom shifted with him, keeping his body between us.

Finally, the assassin cursed. He flung the dagger low, trying to hit me by flinging it past Tom's feet. But the blade wasn't meant for throwing. Unbalanced, it skipped off the floor and bounced to my right, clanging off the fleur-de-lis rail.

Then the man turned and fled.

Everyone, just as shocked as I was, did nothing but stand and watch. The priest who'd shouted was the only one who moved, stepping forward to block the assassin's escape.

He got a fist in the gut for his efforts. The priest bent

over, wheezing. The assassin rammed his elbow behind the priest's ear, then fled, and I lost him in the crowd.

Tom made as if to follow, then thought better of it. He looked around instead. I could almost see the cogs turning behind his eyes. *Was there any more danger?*

When he found nothing, he came and helped me up. "Are you all right?" he said.

I nodded, too rattled to speak. *The King's Men trained him well,* I thought. *He reacted; he was aware.*

And as I stood, it struck me: I *wasn't*. I had two pistols on my belt. I hadn't even thought to draw them.

I remembered a couple of months back, after Lord Ashcombe had rescued us in Devonshire, the King's Men had started training Tom in earnest. One morning, as I watched him spar with Captain Tanner, Tom parried the soldier's attack. He'd stood there, proud of himself—then the King's Man socked him across the face.

You punched me, Tom had said, more shocked than in pain.

The man shrugged. *You let down your guard.*

But . . . we're supposed to be fighting with swords, not fists.

Captain Tanner had shaken his head. *There are no rules in battle, Bailey. A real fight isn't exercises and carefully practiced maneuvers. Your enemy will be unpredictable, and you'll be scared, and you won't have time to think. You'll need to act. Or you'll be dead.*

Tom had learned that lesson well. He'd acted—whereas I'd just sat there like a fool, my two pistols no more useful in my belt than if I'd left them back at Whitehall. If Lord Ashcombe had been here, there'd have been one dead assassin. I imagined him seeing how I'd frozen and thanked God he hadn't been here to watch it. I didn't think I could have lived down the shame.

Master Benedict spoke in my head. *Don't be so hard on yourself. Everything takes practice. And fighting is not your way.*

But I remembered the soldier's lesson. *The assassin didn't care what my way was. And I won't have time to practice, if failing means I'm dead.*

And yet, Master Benedict said, *you learned something. So next time, you* will *act.*

At that moment, it was difficult to believe him.

The crowd milled about us: me, Tom, and the priest on the floor, catching his breath. There were a lot of *are-you-all-right*s, and *yes-I'm-fine*s, and *what-madness-is-this-right-here-in-the-church*s, before everyone more or less left us alone to gossip among themselves. This would be the talk of the town for days.

I picked up the dagger the assassin had left behind. Then Tom and I checked on the priest, who'd got the worst of it. When all three of us said "Are you all right?" at the same time, we laughed, and the shock of the would-be murder finally faded.

The priest rubbed his head where the man had hit him. "Is it always like this?" he said, somewhat sadly. I caught a hint of a French accent. He explained he was on a pilgrimage—to Saint Erkenwald, no less—on behalf of one of his elderly parishioners back home in Rouen.

"It's not," Tom insisted, English pride already wounded. "We're sorry this happened to you."

"Not your fault, *mes amis*. God be with you."

He left, sporting a growing bruise behind his ear, and though we didn't say anything, Tom and I knew the priest was wrong. It *was* our fault.

"I just can't believe it," Tom said. In his own way, he was as shaken as I was. "In Saint Paul's, in broad daylight! How has it come to this?"

It was a good question. I'd begun feeling more and more as if we were trapped. Pinned between two warring factions: the Covenanters on one side, and the Templars on the other. Why were they fighting each other?

And why were they both focused on me?

The Templars were sending me letters. The Covenanters were trying to kill me. If Simon was right, they'd even gone after him just because he was on his way to Blackthorn.

So what made me so important?

I remembered the spymaster's warning. *The human mind is exceptional at recognizing patterns. So good, in fact, that when there* are *no patterns, we invent them to fill the gaps.*

I shook my head. That's exactly what I was doing. I didn't have enough information to answer any of my questions. I didn't even know for sure that it was the Templars and the Covenanters fighting each other.

I did, however, have something new to look at. I pulled the note we'd found on Saint Erkenwald's tomb from my doublet. It had crumpled in the scuffle, but I had no problem reading the initials on the outside.

C. R.

Tom leaned over my shoulder as I opened it to read the message.

Low the swan flies, ever lower;
Dancing, singing overhead,

Slow the song plays, ever slower;
Oh, too late—now they're all dead.

"That's . . . not good," Tom said.

"No," I said, especially because I thought I understood what it was trying to tell me. Not the code, this time. The riddle. And if I was right, we were in terrible trouble.

"What is it?" Tom said.

I folded the note back in my pocket. "We have to get to Isaac's. *Now.*"

CHAPTER
30

WE BARRELED THROUGH THE DOOR
into Isaac's shop.

"Isaac? Sally?"

"Up here," Sally called.

Upstairs, we found Isaac wrapped in a blanket in front of the fire, sipping a half-finished cup of coffee. Sally had one, too, but hers was mostly untouched. Her face was flushed, and she was huffing, from climbing up and down those hundred-plus steps to the secret library, collecting the books Isaac had asked for.

She'd stacked them beside him. I recognized the binding of the larger pile of books. It was a sepia-toned leather:

Master Benedict's journals. There were more books as well, on the floor and the table, where Bridget marched about, happily pecking at some seeds Isaac had scattered for her.

Sally noticed our expressions. "What's wrong?"

"We were attacked," I said.

"*He* was attacked," Tom said—and clearly I was still rattled by what had happened, because it was only then that it really struck me what should have been obvious from the start.

The assassin couldn't have cared less about Tom. It was me he'd wanted to kill.

And again that question: *Why?*

I was hoping Isaac might have an answer. When Tom told them everything that had happened, they were as shocked as we were.

"The brazenness of it," Isaac said, troubled. "It bodes ill."

"Did you find anything?" Sally said.

"There was another riddle on Saint Erkenwald's tomb," I said, distracted. I was still mulling over what I'd first thought about in the church: being in the middle of two warring factions. "Did you find that confession about the Templars?"

"It's there." Isaac nodded toward a paper on the desk beside Sally. She held it out to him, but he waved it away.

"You went to the trouble of getting it, dear. You can read it."

Sally shifted in her chair as Tom and I took seats at the table. "This is from . . . What year was it again?"

"1624," Isaac said. "The last year of the reign of James I. The confession comes from a silk merchant, Jonathan Egerton, who was accused of plotting against the king."

Bridget flapped up to my shoulder as Sally read the note to us, a report from spy to spymaster.

The prisoner Egerton refuses to admit sedition. Instead, he insists he was working on behalf of His Majesty's well-being. In particular, he claims to be a member of the ancient order of the Knights Templar, despite all knowing the order was disbanded three hundred years ago. This imagining could not be dissuaded, even under considerable encouragement.

"He means torture," Isaac said. "Go on."

Sally continued.

I inquired with him as to the precise nature of this supposedly secret sect. In my opinion, Egerton's claims are fanciful, an attempt to explain away his crimes as innocent, or even beneficial. But I must also account to your lordship that Egerton insisted they were the truth, even until death.

He asserts:

The Templars exist, despite their supposed demise.

Their purpose is to work behind the scenes, to shape events, to keep countries stable, and to prevent society from descending into chaos.

Their structure is hierarchical. At the top is the Templar Grand Council, a body of twelve, consisting of eleven knights and one Grand Master.

The Templars work in chapters. Each chapter is responsible for a specific region, usually a major city. The head of each chapter is the Knight Captain.

Each chapter may contain up to a dozen knights, though most are much smaller. In some places, a chapter is a single knight, operating alone.

Each chapter is totally independent. Except for the Knight Captain, the members of one chapter have no knowledge of any in other chapters.

Though generally self-reliant, the Templars occasionally call on agents outside the Brotherhood. These allies can then call upon the Templars for help, if they know how to reach them. Egerton claims their agents can be identified through their possession of a gold coin: a florin, marked by the Templar cross and the name of their original patron, King Baldwin of Jerusalem.

Messages between chapters, knights, and their agents are always enciphered. It is the responsibility of the recipient of the message to know how to decipher the code. By using a cipher, even an intercepted message will offer no information to their enemies.

I asked Egerton how a society that has been extinct for three hundred years was supposed to have enemies. He stated that all who sought to bring chaos were an enemy.

Unfortunately, at this time, Egerton expired, so no more information could be obtained.

Your faithful servant,

J.

We sat in silence for a moment.

"What do you think?" Isaac said.

"I think that man was a Templar," I said. "He knew

about the florin. And the bit about the ciphers fits, too." All three letters I'd got were nothing but riddles and codes.

The stuff about the Grand Council and the independent chapters was new to me, but nothing there contradicted anything we'd learned in Paris. Father Bernard had even hinted at it when he'd confessed he hadn't known for sure where the Templar treasure was. It really did seem to fit together.

Tom was frowning.

"What's wrong?" I said.

"The letter says the Templars send messages through codes."

"Just like the letters I've received."

"Yes, but so far we've just been running around in circles."

"What do you mean?" Sally said.

"Well," Tom said, "the first letter told Christopher to go to the Banqueting House, where we found a second letter. That one told him to go to Saint Paul's, where we found a third letter. But none of the letters have actually *told* us anything. It's just 'go here, now go there.' If it's the Templars leaving those messages, why are they making us run around? They haven't really been helping."

That was a fair point. And yet . . . "I think that's about to change," I said.

"Why?"

"Because I'm pretty sure this third message is a warning."

CHAPTER
31

I PULLED THE CRUMPLED LETTER

from beneath my doublet and spread it on the table. Everyone leaned in to read it.

> *Low the swan flies, ever lower,*
> *Dancing, singing overhead,*
>
> *Slow the song plays, ever slower,*
> *Oh, too late—now they're all dead.*

"You know what this means?" Sally said.

"Part of it," I said, and I turned to Isaac. "Do you remember that key my master left with you for me to find? The first day I came here, last spring?"

"I'm old, Christopher, not senile," he said.

"Right. Sorry. Um . . . that page, with the alchemical symbols. Did my master ever write down any more of them?"

Isaac regarded me for a moment, frowning. Then he turned to Sally. "Did you find that book I asked you to bring up? The one with the blue spine?"

She nodded and pulled it from the stack beside her. He motioned to give it to me.

"Look in there," Isaac said. "You'll find a few pages tucked inside."

I flipped through the book. It was an ordinary work on theology, but pressed between several of the pages were leaves of paper. Each one was covered in symbols, Master Benedict's handwriting beside them, giving definitions.

"This is it," I said.

Sally looked at Isaac, puzzled. "How did you know Christopher would ask for those?"

"The Templar's confession." Isaac finished the last of

his coffee. "Do you remember what poor Mr. Egerton said? 'It is the responsibility of the recipient of the message to know how to decipher the code.' That's only possible if the recipient—in this case, Christopher—already knows what he's looking for.

"The first letter was Vigenère. The second, Alberti's disk. The books I asked you to collect hold many of the ciphers Benedict taught him." Still, he looked troubled.

"What's the matter?" Sally said.

"These Templars," Isaac said slowly, "seem to know quite a bit about Christopher—*and* Benedict. In particular, what Christopher has been taught. I'm not sure how that's possible."

That made me pause. I hadn't really thought too hard about the codes themselves. After what happened in Paris, the Templars would have known I could solve ciphers.

And yet they'd only seen me decipher Vigenère. I'd never used Alberti's disk before, beyond what my master had shown me.

So how did they know I even had the device?

Another question without an answer—and no way of getting one. I forced myself to put it aside for the moment. Instead, I scanned Master Benedict's notes, looking for a particular symbol that matched one in the message.

"How did *you* know what to look for?" Tom asked me. "Have you seen these symbols before?"

"Well . . . the middle glyph does look like an alchemical symbol," I said. "But the real clue was in the riddle. The swan."

"'Low the swan flies,'" Sally said, reading the first line. "What does it mean?"

"It's not talking about a bird. 'Swan' is a reference to a substance apothecaries use. It's called that because, just as a cygnet changes into a swan, this substance can change its appearance completely."

And there it was.

I turned Master Benedict's notes around so they could read it.

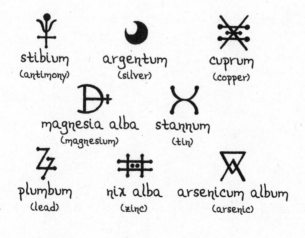

stibium
(antimony)

argentum
(silver)

cuprum
(copper)

magnesia alba
(magnesium)

stannum
(tin)

plumbum
(lead)

nix alba
(zinc)

arsenicum album
(arsenic)

Tom scanned the page until he spotted the right symbol. "'Arsenicum album,'" he read. Then he saw the translation next to it. "But that's . . ."

I nodded. "White arsenic. This message *is* a warning. Someone's about to be poisoned."

CHAPTER
32

TOM WAS HORRIFIED. "WHO?"

"That's what I don't know yet," I said. "The answer has to be in these other two symbols. Or the riddle."

"They're not alchemical?"

"I don't think so. Alchemical symbols are all lines and swirls. These look like they mean something else."

Sally leaned over the message, frowning. Then she looked up, surprised. "Berkshire House."

"What?"

"This." She pointed to the third symbol. It looked like the outline of a mountain, with three diamonds. "I saw it on a banner at Berkshire House."

"Are you sure?"

"Absolutely. It's hanging over the mantel, in the parlor."

"So that means . . . someone will be poisoned at Berkshire House?" Tom said. "But who?"

Whoever the oak leaf referred to, I would guess. "Oak symbolizes a lot of things," I said. "Strength. Long life. Faith. Loyalty. The oak is the king of trees—"

Tom gasped.

"The king!" he said, eyes wide. "What if the oak is the king?"

"Why would it be?" Isaac said.

"Because of the oak where His Majesty hid, to avoid Cromwell's troops. It's why we have Oak Apple Day."

It wasn't surprising that Tom, wearing his hat again, would think of the king first. But there was a certain logic to what he said. What's more, if the Covenanters were our enemy, then they were definitely after Charles. We'd just have to figure out how they'd get him.

Turns out Sally already knew. "Tom's right," she said. "It *is* the king. They're going to try to poison him. And they're going to do it tomorrow."

"How you do know?" I said.

"The riddle. 'Slow the song plays, ever slower, dancing, singing overhead.' What does that sound like?"

"A party," Tom said.

"Remember what I told you when you came to get me? I've been invited to a party. It's tomorrow—at Berkshire House." She tapped the last symbol on the letter. "The king's supposed to attend."

Tom rose. "We have to call it off!"

"No," Isaac said suddenly. "Don't."

We stared at him, puzzled. "But . . . the king!"

"Warn him, yes. But look." With a slight grimace of pain, Isaac leaned forward. "If you cancel the party, you will prevent *this* poisoning. What about the *next* one? How will you stop that?

"This message puts you *ahead* of the Covenanters, do you see? If you say nothing for now, they won't know their plot has been discovered. They'll continue on as usual. So if you use the time to flush them out—"

"We might catch them in the act!" I stood and paced the room. We were ahead of the game, for once. If we played this right . . . we might bring the whole conspiracy down.

"So what's the easiest way to poison someone at a party?" Sally said.

I knew that answer already. "The wine."

We hurried back to Berkshire House.

CHAPTER

"IMPOSSIBLE," THE STEWARD SAID.

We'd ridden to Berkshire House as fast as we could. Leaving our mounts at the stable, we'd hurried inside. Sally had stopped us in the doorway, pointing to the banner over the mantel in the entrance.

"Look."

The third symbol was right there in the heraldry. Confident now that we'd got the riddle right, we'd run straight to the steward, Mr. Dencourt. He was responsible for organizing tomorrow's party. We'd told him we were worried that someone might poison the king.

At first, he'd threatened us with a thrashing for playing pranks. It had taken all our powers of persuasion to convince him we weren't joking—and I doubted we'd have succeeded if he hadn't recognized Sally as the king's new ward. Now he was just dismissive, blaming our fears on overactive imaginations. My holding a pigeon probably didn't help him take us seriously.

"But—" Sally said.

"It simply cannot happen, young lady," Dencourt said. "Our precautions are beyond reproach."

"All it takes is one mistake," I said.

"Which is why we shall make none."

"It's not like it's never happened before."

He was beginning to lose his patience. "If you are referring to the events in Oxford last autumn, that is *exactly* why it won't happen again. Come with me."

He led us into the wine cellar. Four racks stretched into the musty damp, holding hundreds of bottles. He motioned to the rack on the left. A guard, leaning against the wall, snapped to attention as we approached.

"This is the wine for the party," Dencourt said. "As you can see, I have set a man to watch over it. What's more, after the poisoning at Oxford, I have implemented an entirely new system."

He pulled a bottle from the nearest rack and handed it to me.

"First, each bottle is inspected—by me, and me alone—for tampering or defect. If I find none, I stop the cork with wax, and seal it."

He showed me his ring. It was silver, its face engraved with a scrolled *D*—for Dencourt, I assumed. The *D* was pressed into the seal atop the bottle.

"When the party begins," he continued, "I will again inspect the bottle and the seal. If there are no indications of tampering, only then will I pour the wine."

"Couldn't someone put poison in after that?" Sally said.

"Or in the glasses, even," Tom said.

"That still wouldn't harm the king. Because, you see, His Majesty shall drink *only* from the first glass poured from a bottle. And *I* will be the only one to serve him. If a blackguard could somehow intrude on the party—which he could not—then whomever he poisons, I assure you, it will *not* be the king."

Patience finally spent, he shooed us from the cellar. Alone again in the parlor, I had to admit, they'd learned a lot from their mistakes last November. Dencourt's system was as safe as any I could think of.

"Unless Dencourt himself is the assassin," Tom said.

That was possible. But now we were jumping at shadows. "So that's it?" Sally said. "The Templars' warning was false?"

"Well . . . we haven't checked the food yet," I said.

Tom was always up for a trip to a kitchen. "What are they serving?"

I shrugged. "Let's find out."

I shut Bridget in Sally's room—I didn't like the idea of leaving a plump little bird around cooks with large knives—before heading off to the kitchens. The cook we spoke to was a lot nicer than the steward. Sally made things even easier by not mentioning poison. Instead, she pretended His Majesty had sent her to ask what there'd be to eat.

"Here you go, miss," he said, and he handed her a long and detailed list.

The kitchens had planned a spread on several tables. The list looked like the usual: meat, cheese, bread, sweets, and pastry.

"Can these be cooked with poison?" Sally asked quietly.

"Master Benedict said arsenic works best fresh," I said. "I think you'd want to sprinkle it on after it was finished."

"Wouldn't that be noticed?"

Probably. Master Benedict's notes explained that, in France, where arsenic was popular, a poisoner would usually mix it into someone's plate. But from the looks of the menu, there wouldn't be individual servings. Just finished dishes on the table, from which the patrons could take what they liked. Tom studied the list as Sally spoke.

"Would you be able to taste the poison?" Sally asked.

"No," I said. "Arsenic has no taste. No smell, either. It's why it's used so much. If you can find some way of hiding it, your victim will never even know they were poisoned. The effects look the same as cholera. A lot of people have probably died thinking it was just an illness."

"It has no taste?" Tom said, frowning at the list.

"None."

"So if you mixed it in with something else?"

"It would taste like whatever it was mixed with. Why?"

He looked up, still frowning. "You called it *white* arsenic before. But is it actually white?"

"Yes, it's a white powder. What are you getting at?"

"Here." He showed us the list, pointing to the desserts and pastries at the bottom. "The cream puffs."

"What about them?"

Tom, the baker's son, had spotted what we'd missed. "You finish them off by dusting them with powdered sugar."

Powdered sugar. White—just like arsenic. The assassin could mix it in at any time. And then . . .

Death by cream puff. Tom took that personally.

"What do we do?" Sally said.

"Warn the king," Tom insisted. "And cancel the party."

We'd warn the king, certainly. But as for canceling the party, Isaac's point still stood. "Maybe we can catch the traitors in the act."

"You think they'll slip the poison in tomorrow?" Sally said. "If the cook watches the food as closely as Mr. Dencourt watches the wine, I don't see how they wouldn't be caught."

That was a good point. Which made me wonder something else.

"How did the Templars know the king would be poisoned with arsenic?" I said.

"I thought the Templars knew everything," Tom said.

"They can't know *everything*. They might have agents in high places, but they're still just people."

"What are you thinking?" Sally said.

"The servant at Whitehall who was murdered, Mary Brickenham. She worked in the kitchens. What if she was killed because she saw someone doing something strange?"

"Like putting something in the food!"

"Maybe. Either way, Whitehall's on edge now. So what if the Covenanters had planned to poison the king at the palace, but had to move their plot here, to Berkshire House, instead?"

"All right," Tom said. "And?"

"Well . . . what if they don't plan to poison the food the night of the party? *What if the poison's already here?* In the pantry, in the powdered sugar, say. Then it wouldn't matter who's watching for danger. The sugar's already poisoned. The cook will do the assassin's work for him, without even knowing it."

We stood there, struck by the deviousness.

"Come on," I said. "We need to check the kitchen's stores."

CHAPTER
34

THE SERVANTS THOUGHT US ODD,
going into the pantry. "Dinner be served in half an hour,
yer graces," one of the kitchen maids said.

I told her the master had sent us to check on some supplies. She found that dubious, but she wasn't bold enough
to challenge us. Inside the pantry, Tom went straight for the
sacks of powdered sugar.

"We should take these," he insisted, so no one could get
poisoned, even by accident.

"Do you know of any way to test for arsenic?" Sally
asked me.

"Only one," I said, and I went back out to the maid in the kitchen. "Are there any rats?"

She looked at me strangely. "It's lamb tonight, m'lord."

"I . . . wasn't looking for something to eat. I need them alive."

Her look didn't change much. "Always some in the storage cellar. If you can catch 'em."

"Working for the king certainly is glamorous," Tom said. He was on his knees, peering under one of the shelves near the wall. "Here, rat, rat, rat."

I was on the other side of the storage cellar, my head to the floor. "I don't think that's going to work," I said, looking into the shadows.

"Maybe if we trick them. Look, Mr. Rat, I have cheese." His voice sounded muffled all of a sudden.

"Tom?"

"Yffgh?"

"Are you eating the cheese?"

" . . . No."

I glared at him across the cellar. "You're talking to the cook if we run out."

"It was just a little piece! How much cheese does a rat need, anyway? I'm bigger than he is."

"Maybe that's because you eat everything you see."

"It's not my fault I'm hungry! We're always chasing death—can't we stop just once to have lunch?"

Sally shook her head. "I can't believe the king put his life in the hands of you two."

"You're one to talk," Tom said. "We're on our knees in the damp, on hard stone! All you're doing is holding a lantern. Like the light is going to bring them running."

"Oh, I'm sorry. Is this better?"

She slipped the hood over the lantern, plunging the cellar into total darkness.

"How am I supposed to find a rat now?" Tom complained.

"Try eating more cheese—see if that works."

I'd had enough. "I swear to the angels high in heaven, I am trying to find a poisoner here. If you two want to keep playing the goat—"

I froze.

Sally pulled the hood from the lantern. "Did you see a rat?"

"Shadow that light," I whispered. "Shadow it!"

Once again, the room fell into darkness.

I let my eyes adjust for a moment. Then I stared across the cellar.

"Look," I said. "Over there."

Tom's whisper came from the black. "You realize we can't see where you're pointing, right?"

"The wall, opposite the door."

Silence. "I still don't see anything," he began, but then he fell quiet, too.

On the far side, where there should have been nothing but shelves, there was light. Just a sliver, a thin line rising from the floor, almost to the ceiling.

"The lantern," I said.

Sally removed the hood again. The lantern's glare wasn't much, but it was enough to cause the light to fade from sight.

"I thought this and the wine cellar were the only rooms underground," I said.

Sally looked at me. "So did I."

We moved closer. Against the wall were three shelves, each full of folded linens and old kitchen utensils. I motioned for Sally to step off to the right. She kept the lantern shining, but up close, with the shadows cast by the wood, I could make out the light again, all along the left side of the center shelf.

"A secret door," I said. There had to be a passage behind it. "Look for a latch."

Sally put the lantern down and joined us as we fumbled around the wall. We poked at the shelves, behind the linens, into the bricks, the mortar between them. Finally, Tom found it.

There was a lever up high, above the middle shelf. He pulled it.

Clack.

The shelf came forward an inch, grinding against the stone underneath. Light bright enough to see even in the lantern's glow made a vertical line in the wall.

Tom grabbed the shelf and pulled it the rest of the way. Its hinges creaked, echoing deafeningly in the cellar.

And that's when they attacked us.

CHAPTER

ALL I SAW WAS A SILHOUETTE.

It came at me from the passage, suddenly in my face. I reacted this time: I reached for my pistols. I just managed to get a palm on one of the grips.

Then an elbow smashed me in the jaw.

Pain shot through my cheek, and I tasted the copper of blood. As my head snapped to the side, I lost control of my legs and sprawled onto my back.

I scrabbled to get away, panicking. A weight landed on me, a body, shoving me down. Strong hands grabbed my arms, then pinned them, crushing my wrists under armored knees. A hand covered my face and pushed, cracking the back of my skull into the stone. I saw stars.

Tom shouted in alarm and drew his sword. Sally squealed, tripping over her own feet as she backpedaled, landing hard some distance away. Her heel clipped the lantern; it rattled as it spun, teetering on its edge before finally deciding to topple. The glass cracked, and there was a flare of light as the oil in the ampoule ignited in the flame.

Fire, I thought dumbly, barely able to form any thoughts at all. Tom was already moving forward, as more silhouettes advanced from the secret passage.

The broad blade of a halberd thrust toward him. With Eternity freed from its sheath, Tom slashed downward. His sword lopped the end of the halberd off its pole, sending the blade clattering across the stone. A second stroke upward sent the next three feet of the halberd's pole flying into the darkness. The man holding the weapon cursed in alarm and fell back. Eternity rang with a song of holy triumph.

Then the edge of a blade bit into my neck, and my thoughts returned with terrified clarity. Another halberd was thrust in Tom's direction. A voice, harsh and biting, cut through the fight.

"Hold!"

The sword at my neck obeyed, the edge barely slicing

my skin. The new halberd stopped its advance. Tom stood ready, his grip two-handed, Eternity held low, point high.

"Drop your—" the voice commanded, but it cut off, returning with surprise. "You?"

The man who'd shouted stepped from the passage. As he came into the light, I saw his livery.

He was one of the King's Men.

From his insignia, he was a captain. In his hand he gripped a sword, but only half ready. He was staring at Tom, who still stood in a defensive stance.

"I know you," the captain said. Then he spoke to his comrades—four of them, King's Men all. "This one came back with the general," he said, meaning Lord Ashcombe. "The girl, too. What are you doing here?"

Tom was confused. He knew we weren't supposed to tell anyone what we were doing, but he also hadn't expected to cross swords with the King's Men. He looked to me, uncertain.

The soldier who held me pinned still had his blade at my throat. This wasn't the time to be cagey.

"We're following orders from Lord Ashcombe," I said. "We're here by his command."

"I very much doubt that," the captain said.

"That's why we're in the cellar," I said. "We didn't know about . . . that."

I couldn't motion my head toward the secret passage without getting cut, but the captain understood my meaning. "What's your name?" he said to Tom.

Tom looked at me. I nodded—carefully. "Tom Bailey."

"Well, then, Bailey, how about you drop that sword?"

Tom's grip tightened on the hilt, uncertain. "Let Christopher go."

The captain considered this. Then he nodded to the man on top of me.

The King's Man pulled his blade away, though my arms remained squashed under his knees. Tom lowered his sword, and the captain followed suit.

"On the ground," the captain said. "Kick it to me."

Tom hesitated, but again I nodded, and he did as commanded. The captain picked up Eternity, surprised at its brilliance.

"Well, now," he said. "This is going to be interesting."

The King's Men hoisted me from the floor. I was quickly stripped of my pistols. They searched me and Tom for more weapons, taking our knives and the assassin's dagger, then removing my apothecary sash, again with some surprise at what was inside. They didn't put their hands on Sally, but they ordered her to sit with us, while two of the men kept watch.

The captain—name of Clemens, he said—dumped linens on the fire from the broken lantern. Fortunately, there hadn't been much oil left, so it smothered quickly, leaving the cellar in a smoky haze. Then he turned to us.

"Tell me what you're really doing here," he said.

I rubbed my arms, all prickly with pins and needles. "I'm not allowed."

"You realize we could just cut you down and dump your bodies in the park?"

I tried to keep the fear off my face. "Lord Ashcombe wouldn't like that very much. You saw Tom and Sally with him, didn't you?"

"Don't mean you're still in his good graces."

"Then go speak to him." My voice softened. "Please. Tell him you found Christopher Rowe doing . . . whatever it is you think I'm doing. What's the harm in that?"

He thought about it. "Perkin. Off you go."

Perkin was the man whose polearm had been chopped into pieces. He was apparently still sour about it, because his answer was surly. "I'm taking orders from children now?"

"No, you're taking orders from me. But while you're there, tell the general you don't like following commands no more. See how fast he cracks your teeth."

Perkin left. Captain Clemens regarded me curiously but didn't ask me anything else. Instead, he spoke to Tom. "Bailey, was it? You sure know how to use this sword."

Tom perked up, pleased. "You mean it?"

"Made short enough work of Perkin's halberd."

"Captain Tanner taught me that in Brighton," Tom said proudly.

Clemens got a faraway look in his eyes. He didn't say anything, but I could almost read his mind. *Tanner was in Brighton with the general. And I've seen that technique before.*

He turned to Sally. "And you, young miss. You all right? You took a nasty fall there."

She shrugged. "I've had worse."

"I suppose you trained with Tanner, too? Or maybe you're a princess in disguise."

"I'm hardly His Majesty's daughter," she said. "I'm just his ward."

The captain studied her carefully. "One of us is going to be in big trouble when all this is over," he said, "and I'm starting to think it might be me."

He didn't ask anything more after that, just leaned back against the shelf that had hid the secret door, lost in thought. I took the opportunity to glance past him, into the passage.

I couldn't see much from where I sat, but I could tell it wasn't just a tunnel. There was a small area, where the King's Men had been waiting, lit by three lanterns hanging from rusted hooks. In the center was a table, a cup, a pair of dice, and some pennies; they'd been gambling to pass the time. Beyond that, I saw a passage stretching off to the south. No lanterns lit that corridor, so I couldn't see too far down, but I did spot an iron door in one wall, fixed shut with three giant padlocks.

It left me burning with curiosity. What had they been doing in there?

I knew better than to ask.

It took some time for Perkin to return. When he did, he looked even more sour than before. "The general says bring them to Whitehall."

Captain Clemens nodded. "And their weapons?"

"Says give them back."

"I have to get my pigeon upstairs, too," I said.

Clemens stared at me, then laughed. He was still chuckling as he handed us our things. "Come find me sometime, Bailey. We'll spar."

"Yes, sir," Tom said, beaming.

The captain gave me an ironic salute as Tom collected the sacks of sugar we'd taken from the kitchen. Perkin escorted us out.

I figured we'd be taken to Lord Ashcombe's office. Instead, Perkin brought us to the door of the parlor where we'd been this morning, two men with halberds standing guard. Sally hadn't been with us, so she didn't understand what this meant. Tom did. He turned pale.

One of the guards knocked on the door as we approached. A moment later, Lord Ashcombe opened it. He glared at the three of us, then pointed to Tom and Sally.

"You. Sit."

They did.

He pointed to me.

"You. In here."

I handed Bridget to Sally. Sally's expression said, *Sorry this is happening.* Tom's said, *This is all your fault.*

CHAPTER

HIS MAJESTY AWAITED ME IN THE parlor. Like this morning, he had a glass of wine in his hand, though there were only half as many spaniels in the room. Three of them ran up to me, tails wagging. One of them was Barbara, looking at me again with hopeful eyes. Given Lord Ashcombe's expression, I didn't dare pet her.

To my surprise, Walsingham, the spymaster, was also there, in the same chair in which I'd sat this morning. He watched me without acknowledgment, expression unreadable.

Charles looked both exasperated and amused. "Here's trouble," he said. "Odd's fish, Christopher, you have the most remarkable ability to end up where you shouldn't."

I noticed I wasn't invited to sit this time. Lord Ashcombe loomed over me. "Explain yourself."

I still didn't really understand what I'd done wrong. "My lord?"

"What were you doing in the Berkshire House cellar?"

"We were . . . uh . . . looking for a rat."

"A *rat*?"

The king laughed. "Oh, this I have to hear."

I told them everything. About solving the puzzle with Walsingham this morning, then finding the second riddle in the Banqueting House. I explained how that had led us to Saint Paul's, and how I'd been attacked. I gave Lord Ashcombe the assassin's dagger, then showed them all the final letter, and what we thought it meant: that the king was to be poisoned at tomorrow night's party with arsenic, which had already been mixed with the powdered sugar. Probably.

They all exchanged silent glances.

"Where is this sugar now?" Lord Ashcombe said.

"Tom has it, outside, my lord."

"So what was the rat for?"

Before I could answer, the spymaster spoke, in his soft, quiet voice. "To test if the sugar is poisoned."

He stood and went to the door. Opening it, he spoke to

one of the waiting servants, who brought the sacks in from Tom. The spaniels sniffed around him.

"The dogs, sire," Walsingham said.

Charles understood. If one of them licked poisoned sugar . . . He ordered the guards to usher the spaniels out. The servant placed the sacks on the table and, after a quiet word from Walsingham, left.

"You don't expect me to eat it, I hope?" the king said.

"A rat is coming," the spymaster said.

I decided to chance asking. "M—" I caught myself just before saying Master. "My lord?"

Walsingham raised an eyebrow.

"Did we do something wrong? I don't understand why everyone is so cross."

"I'm not cross," he said.

Lord Ashcombe snorted.

"Tell me," the spymaster said, "what you think happened."

"Well . . . we stumbled—*totally by accident*," I emphasized, "on that secret passage. I'm assuming there's something in there we weren't supposed to see. Or even know about. Behind the iron door with all the locks."

The king drained his glass of wine. "I'm *so* glad you're on my side," he said wryly. "Go on, tell him."

"The passage is an escape tunnel," Lord Ashcombe said. "It exits into a grove in Saint James's Park. It was built during the Civil Wars, in case the house ever came under siege. Several of the homes around here have them, including the palace. As for the vault . . ."

He looked to the king for approval. Charles finished the sentence himself. "It's a secret treasury. There's quite a bit of jewelry in there at the moment, some forty thousand pounds' worth."

I glanced over at the spymaster. He said nothing, and his expression remained as blank as ever. But I was sure he was thinking the same thing I was.

They have guards going in and out of the cellar all day long. The guards know. The servants almost certainly know, too. So how secret can this vault be?

It probably wasn't my place to say anything, but I did anyway. "With respect, sire . . . if we found it, couldn't anyone?"

Walsingham nodded at me, barely a shift of the head. He approved. Before the others could respond, he said, "Who is sending you these letters?"

The change of subject caught me off guard, confused me for a moment. I wondered if that was his intention.

The Templars, I thought. I almost said it. But this was

a secret *I'd* promised to keep. I had to lie. Sort of.

"I don't know," I said. Which wasn't, technically, a lie. I *didn't* know. I just believed.

"Who do you think?" Walsingham said.

His voice remained quiet, even as he pressed me. *He knows,* I thought. *He already knows.*

And then I thought: *What if he's a Templar?*

Egerton's confession had claimed the Templars kept agents of their own close to the king. It was hard to get closer than spymaster. Unless you considered . . .

No. Couldn't be.

I glanced over at Lord Ashcombe. He, too, waited for my response.

My mind was running away with theories. I had to answer the question. I couldn't tell the literal truth this time, so I settled for half of it.

"Whoever's sending the letters," I said carefully, "knows far too much about the king's enemies to be an outsider. He must have infiltrated their group. A loyalist, maybe?"

Walsingham's gaze was inscrutable. *He's going to keep pressing me,* I thought.

To my surprise, he didn't. Instead, he asked me something else.

CHAPTER
37

"WHO, THEN," WALSINGHAM SAID, "are His Majesty's enemies?"

I let out a breath. This I could answer. "I think they're Covenanters."

The king scowled at the name. He looked to his spymaster, whose eyes lingered on me a moment more.

"I agree," Walsingham said.

"Let them scheme," Charles spat, all humor gone. "I will never fulfill that oath. I'll burn Scotland to the ground before I submit."

"The Covenanters are aware of that. Which is why they are coming for you."

"Our armies will crush them."

"They're not fighting our armies," Lord Ashcombe pointed out. "They're attacking us from inside."

Speaking of which . . . "My lord?" I said.

Lord Ashcombe turned to me.

"Do you remember when we arrived at the palace yesterday?" I said. "A man shouted at you?"

"Niall Ramsay, Earl of Fife. What of him?"

"The man who was with him. The one wearing gold spectacles. Do you know who he is?"

"Domhnall Ardrey. He's the Baron of Oxton. Why?"

"He was in the Banqueting House yesterday."

Lord Ashcombe's eye bored into me. "Doing what?"

"I don't know," I said. "He came in with a letter of his own, already opened. It looked like he was planning to meet someone. But he got spooked and left."

"What happened to the letter?" Walsingham asked.

"He burned it."

Lord Ashcombe turned to His Majesty. "Arrest him."

"For what?" the spymaster asked quietly.

"Being Scottish."

The king laughed.

"It would be a mistake, sire," Walsingham said.

"I know, I know," Charles said. "More fuel to the fire."

"Not my point. If Ardrey is a Covenanter, as long as he doesn't know we've tumbled him, we have an advantage."

"What do you suggest?"

"I'll put a man on him. Follow—ah."

A knock on the door signaled the return of one of the servants. He'd found a rat somewhere. He carried the animal in a cage, which he placed on the table at Walsingham's instruction. After he left, the spymaster spooned a pile of powdered sugar between the bars. The rat sniffed at it and began to eat.

"It's not dying," the king said.

"Depending on the dose," Walsingham said, "it may take some time for the poison to work."

"Am I supposed to sit here and wait?"

"What do you think we should do next?"

It took me a moment to realize Walsingham was asking me. I was startled. "You want *me* to decide?"

"His Majesty will decide. I asked for a course of action."

I flushed. "Of course. Sorry." Lord Ashcombe was already growing impatient; I hurried along. "I think we have a big problem. The first letter I got told us the Covenanters are after the king. And the two murdered servants make it clear: They've already infiltrated the palace."

"Have you discovered why the girls were killed?" the king asked curiously.

"Not for sure. But . . . well, this is something Sally pointed out when we went to Paris. Nobody ever pays attention to servants. They come and go as if they're invisible, because—er . . . forgive me, sire—no one thinks they're important enough to matter.

"But they see and hear *everything*. That's what I think: The murdered girls saw something they shouldn't have. Someone trying to poison your food at Whitehall, maybe. The killer got rid of the girls, but now the palace is on alert. So they found another way to get to you. There's a party scheduled for tomorrow at Berkshire House, so they moved the plot to kill you across the park.

"Here's the problem," I continued. "Someone had to poison all this sugar. How could they do this? There are guards all over the place, and servants are almost always in the kitchen. It should have been hard to get this poison in. But it wasn't. That can mean only one thing: *The Covenanters have already infiltrated Berkshire House, too.*"

Charles frowned. "How is that possible?"

It looked as if he was still asking me. "Um . . . again,

with the greatest respect, sire, that's the easy part. The plague must have killed many of the old servants. The steward would be desperate to hire new ones. If the Covenanters brought forged references—that's how the Raven infiltrated Maison Chastellain—they'd have been hired, no question. With the chaos around the sickness, the steward wouldn't have bothered to check if those references were good."

Charles looked at Walsingham.

"The analysis is sound," the spymaster said.

"But that means nowhere is safe," the king protested.

"Yes," Lord Ashcombe said. "So we move again, out of London."

Charles's face darkened. "Absolutely not."

"Sire—"

"This has been a terrible year. Hardest of all for this city. I cannot abandon my people. Some have already begun to blame me for bringing the plague. They say I've fallen from God's favor. If I flee London so soon after I returned, their faith will collapse."

Lord Ashcombe shrugged. "Better than a dagger in the back."

"No. It is not." The king stood, towering over us all. "My crown lies as precarious as ever. If it falls . . . I promise you, Richard, I will die before I leave England. I will never be exiled again."

And Lord Ashcombe, who had stayed with his king for those miserable years, couldn't help but understand. Death might be acceptable. Humiliation? Never.

"In that case," he said, "we must still remove you from the palace."

"And go where?" Walsingham said. "If Berkshire House is full of enemies, we must assume everywhere in London will be."

"Not everywhere. There's Hampton Court."

The king made a face. "I loathe Hampton."

"I know. And so does everyone else."

It was, in fact, common knowledge that the king hated the place, and with good reason. Hampton Court was where Oliver Cromwell had lived while Charles was doomed to exile.

"Hampton," Lord Ashcombe said, "is where no one expects you to go. So it's less likely the Covenanters will have bothered to infiltrate it."

"It's still outside the city," Charles noted.

"Fourteen miles. Close enough. We'll say you wanted

to go hunting. No one will fault you for that."

The king looked to Walsingham. Slowly, the spymaster nodded. "I agree."

"I swore I'd never go there." Then the king smirked, half to himself. "Odd's fish. I've broken so many oaths; what's one more? We leave tonight, then?"

"Yes," Lord Ashcombe said.

"No." The spymaster shook his head. "If we leave tonight, it will tip off our conspirators. Leave *tomorrow* night, heading for the party as expected. Reroute to Hampton Court instead."

Lord Ashcombe agreed that would work. The king sighed. He reached for his glass, then stopped. "Will somebody remove this blasted rat?"

Walsingham carried the cage himself. Outside the king's parlor, he motioned for me to follow him—then turned sharply and walked over to where Tom and Sally waited nervously.

He looked Sally up and down. "Your mind is astute," he said. Then he spun on his heel and walked off. I glanced at her as I followed; she looked thoroughly confused.

Definitely strange, this man. Though I think I knew what

he'd meant: He'd liked Sally's observation about servants.

I assumed we were going back to his office. Instead, he stopped halfway down some passage and stepped into an open door. It was someone's parlor; a maid was in there scrubbing the floor. She stood and curtsied as we entered.

Walsingham gave her the barest hint of a smile. "Out," he said, though not unkindly.

She hurried away. He shut the door. "Your performance today has been satisfactory."

I remembered what Lord Ashcombe had said. High praise, indeed.

"Thank you, M—" I kept wanting to call him Master. It struck me that maybe it was because, for the first time since Master Benedict had died, I truly felt like an apprentice again. "My lord. I think we have a good plan."

"It will never work."

That surprised me. "Why not?"

"Nothing around the king remains a secret." Walsingham stared at the portrait that hung over the mantel. "His Majesty moves with an entourage. Nobles, guards, servants. The staff at Hampton Court will be alerted; they will need to prepare the house for his arrival."

"Can't we just not tell anyone until the last minute?"

"I can wait to give instructions to the servants. Ashcombe can handle the guards. But no one will silence the nobles. Or the king, for that matter."

"He's not taking this seriously."

"Don't judge him so harshly," Walsingham said. My face grew hot; I hadn't meant to criticize the king. But the spymaster wasn't taking me to task; he was explaining. "His Majesty must be a king not merely in name, but in deed. He cannot appear frightened. If he does—ever—he may as well throw away his crown."

I suppose I understood. "So . . . do we go with His Majesty tomorrow night?"

"No. Ashcombe will escort the king. I will remain in London. You will wait."

"For what?"

"I will task an agent to watch Domhnall Ardrey, Niall Ramsay, and the rest of his Scottish friends," Walsingham said. "Whether they are Covenanters or not, there is a traitor in the palace. As for you, I suspect whoever has been sending you letters is not finished. Do you play chess?"

He had a knack for throwing me off guard. "I—not

really. Master Benedict showed me the rules, but we didn't play much, and Tom's never been interested."

"I will play you, when this game of poisons is finished. But it is *not* finished, apprentice, not yet. Mark my words: The final move will be made tomorrow. Let us pray we do not lose our king."

FRIDAY, MARCH 5, 1666

Et tu, Brute! Then fall, Caesar!

CHAPTER
38

I COULDN'T SLEEP.

My mind kept running through the meeting I'd just had: first in the king's parlor, then with the spymaster, alone. It was mad to think such powerful people were relying on me.

The choices weren't mine; I understood that well enough. But the Templars had still used me to warn His Majesty.

Like a tool, I thought, and I remembered something Master Benedict had once said. It was the first real lesson he'd ever taught me. *It's never the tool that decides. It's the hand—and the heart—of the one who wields it.*

Now *I* was the thing being wielded. By the Templars, by Walsingham, by the king. Master Benedict would argue that, as the tool, I wasn't responsible. The spymaster had already said the same. Yet I couldn't shake that weight from my shoulders. What I'd got myself involved in was not just important, but IMPORTANT; the kind of events they write about in the histories.

And so, in March of Anno Domini 1666, Charles II, the Merry Monarch, was cut down, murdered cruelly by men of the Covenant. So then did the kingdoms of England and Scotland fall once more into war, brother against brother, until blood painted the streets. The failure to protect His Majesty was the failure of one: Christopher Rowe, apprentice.

I hadn't confessed any of this to Tom or Sally. After Walsingham had let me go, I'd led them into the Privy Garden, so no one else could hear. There, among the flowers and statues, I told them what had been decided.

Neither one looked as if they felt themselves responsible. I wished I felt the same.

"So what do we do?" Tom said.

"We wait," I said, echoing the spymaster. "Though I need to go back to Blackthorn early in the morning."

Tom looked at me dubiously. "How early?"

"First light."

"Oh, come on. Why?"

"I want to check on Simon."

"I thought Lord Walsingham said you were supposed to wait for something to happen."

"He did. He just didn't say wait *here*."

Tom groaned. He was already sore from riding around all day, to say nothing of the fights in Saint Paul's and the Berkshire House cellar. He'd been hoping to sleep in.

"You don't have to go," I told him.

"Of course he does," Sally said. "After what happened at the cathedral? Don't be ridiculous."

"We won't be long," I promised him. "It's not just about Simon, anyway. I still need to gather Master Benedict's journals for Isaac." I'd hoped to take them to Isaac myself, but there were too many books to carry by horse, which meant I'd need a cart or carriage. That would take a lot longer to move through the city's traffic. And that really was pushing the whole waiting thing too far.

"I'll take care of the journals," Sally said.

"You don't mind?"

"Not at all. I'll take a carriage from Berkshire House.

Just set the books out in the shop before you leave. I was thinking of visiting Isaac, anyway."

"You don't have to do that."

"I want to. I like him—he's a sweet old man. Funny, too, once you get to know him. He needs someone to look after him, and I have the time. Nothing but time, really." She looked away, hesitating. "Besides, I know how much he means to you."

I studied her for a moment, remembering what Tom had said he wanted in a wife. A kind girl, who'd make a kind home.

She looked so pretty in the torchlight.

"Thank you," I said, and she left for the night. I avoided Tom's grin all the way back to our room.

Tired of lying in bed and not sleeping, I decided to go back to Blackthorn early, before the sun rose. Tom woke as I stuck my pistols in my belt.

"Hnh? Wazzuh ngh?" he said.

"Time to go."

"Mnnnghh," he said, but he did get up. Bleary-eyed, he followed me to the stables. Even the groom on duty was snoozing, sitting on a barrel, slumped against a post.

Blossom nickered as I called her name. She stuck her

head out of her stall to greet me and Bridget, snuffling at both of us. Bridget flew to the top of the stall, then down to land on the horse's back, near her mane.

Blossom turned her head to get a good look at her new rider, decided this was all right, then began nibbling the buttons of my doublet. I rubbed her neck and fed her a pear I'd swiped from last night's dinner. She really was an amazing animal.

"You said first light," Tom complained.

"I know."

"I don't see *any* light."

"I know, I know. Let's just go."

"Odd's fish."

"You have the king's hat," I said. "I don't think you can take his curses, too."

Tom looked guilty, like he'd been caught dipping his hand in the sweets.

We rode quickly, carrying lanterns to light our way. The streets were quiet, too early for traffic, so it took us no time at all to reach Blackthorn. Even Henri, Simon's bodyguard, was sleeping, flat on the counter, arms dangling down. We could hear his snoring from outside.

Simon was already awake, lying on his stomach as usual, chest bandaged. He squinted at our lanterns as we entered my bedroom. "What is it—oh. Christopher," Simon said. "I thought you were Dr. Kemp."

"Does he usually come this early?" I said.

"No. You had me worried for a second. Why are you here at this hour?"

Tom slumped his head against the doorjamb. "Yes, why?" he said.

"I needed to arrange a few things," I said. "And I wanted to check on you."

"Thoughtful of you. I'm all right, other than not sleeping. And being bored out of my mind."

I regretted not being able to be here for him. He wouldn't have any trouble sleeping on the poppy, but once it wore off, the pain would keep him up. "Must be hard, being stuck in bed."

"Even rising to use the chamber pot is an adventure in pain. What's happening at the palace?"

"I'm not really supposed to say."

He rolled a bit, to look at me. "Aha. A secret— Ow!" He rolled back, thinking better of it. "In Paris, that would make you the most interesting man in the room."

"I'd rather be the most boring," I said.

"Take it from me, you wouldn't. Speaking of which, I don't suppose you could find me something among these books, could you? The ones in arm's reach are all apothecary business and philosophy, and while I find it fascinating, I'd rather read something that lets me escape this lovely prison."

I knew just the thing. I scrounged around in the spare room for a moment before I found what I was looking for. By the time I got back, Tom had sat at the desk, head down. I think he was already asleep.

I placed the books on the bed beside Simon. There were two volumes, squat but thick. "Here you go."

Simon stared at them, not moving.

"Something wrong?" I said.

He reached out, touched one of the volumes. His fingers traced over the spine. When he opened the book, he turned to the title page. Homer's *Odyssey*, in Latin and Greek.

"Master Benedict gave this to me," he said quietly.

"He did?"

Simon saw my confusion. "Not this copy. A different set, back in Paris, so many years ago." He cleared his throat. "I told you how I used to hang about his workshop, in Uncle Marin's cellar, when I was eight. I was always pestering him

with questions. Well, one day I begged him to tell me a story. He gave me this. No doubt he thought it would keep me out from underfoot for a while."

He stayed quiet for a moment. Then he whispered, *"Dream of Odysseus, child. Dream of coming home."*

"What's that?" I said.

"Nothing," Simon said. He sounded sad and a little bit angry. "Just something Master Benedict said to me, once. Thank you for bringing this. It's a nice memory."

I was slightly confused by his reaction, until I remembered that his uncle, Marin, whom Simon had lived with as a child, was dead—murdered by the Raven. Simon had never got his revenge.

Which reminded me: I had another job to do here. In the spare rooms, I gathered what I could find of Master Benedict's old journals and piled them in the workshop downstairs, setting water to boil for Simon's poppy.

While rooting around, I found the old chessboard Master Benedict had taught me to play on, tucked away among his other old things. All the pieces were there, so I left it out in the workshop next to the journals. If Walsingham really meant to play me, I should probably refresh my memory of the rules. Maybe Simon would like a game, too, when all this was over.

But that would have to wait. Finished, I collected Bridget and roused Tom. It was time to go back to Whitehall; gathering the journals had taken longer than I'd planned. We said our goodbyes to Simon, who'd already begun to read the *Odyssey*. His good cheer returned; he drank the poppy I'd made gratefully. Then we hopped on our horses and rode back to the palace.

And so, as the spymaster had commanded, we waited. Tom flopped on his bed while I lay on mine, playing with Bridget, worried about everything. The morning passed, and then the afternoon, until Sally arrived.

She reported both Simon and Isaac were in good spirits, if not exactly well. She'd taken a carriage from Berkshire House, and the driver had helped her transfer the journals. Isaac had already started on them and would work through the collection in time.

"Did you send me flowers?" she said suddenly.

I flushed. Tom found something very interesting to study outside the window.

"There was a girl," I said. "She was poor . . . she needed . . . I hired her."

"That was so thoughtful."

"Yes . . . well. Good. Fine."

Tom's shoulders were shaking, which made my face grow even hotter. Sally didn't appear to notice. She just curled up in one of the chairs, pulled out a couple of needles and yarn, and started knitting. She hummed a pleasant tune, smiling to herself.

Other than feeling the fool, all was well. As my embarrassment faded, I almost hoped for some sort of problem, because then at least I'd have something to do. Tom practiced his sword drills. Sally enjoyed her knitting; now that her injured hand had started to recover, she could manipulate the needles again, even if it was slow going.

That left me with nothing. I thought I might practice with my pistols, but both Tom and Sally pointed out—rather forcefully—that maybe firing guns around the palace was not the wisest thing to do at the moment. I was insulted; obviously I wasn't going to shoot them *in* Whitehall. I figured I'd fire into the Thames. Tom told me if even one of my bullets went into the water, I was going in after it.

So the wait was killing me. I should have brought the chessboard. Both Lords Walsingham and Ashcombe were busy with their own preparations for the king's departure to Hampton Court, and it wasn't my place to stick my nose in, so I couldn't learn anything from them. The spymaster was kind enough to remember to send a note I'd been expecting, which was simple and unsigned.

C — The rat died.

In some way, that was a relief. On the one hand, the sugar *had* been poisoned, which was terrible. On the other, we'd saved everyone at the party, and I was spared from looking a complete idiot. Now I wished something would *happen*, already.

I should have wished for anything else.

The letter came after dark.

I didn't see it arrive. I was looking out the window over the Thames, watching the torchlight and lanterns glow over the ripples in the water, when Sally suddenly stopped humming.

"Where did that come from?"

She'd paused in mid-yarn-loop. She stared, head cocked, at a small beige rectangle on the rug near the door.

I nearly fell off my chair scrambling to get it. Lord Walsingham was right. I'd got a letter. *C. R.* on the front, the back sealed with a circle in red wax. My heart skipped a beat as I cracked it open and read the message inside.

The name of the enemy. Leave it with the flowers.

Come alone.

CHAPTER

"NOT A CHANCE," TOM SAID.

"This is what Lord Walsingham ordered me to wait for," I said.

"I don't care. No. A thousand times no."

Sally agreed with him. "You can't go alone, Christopher. You remember what happened the last time you were at Saint Paul's."

What the letter commanded was simple enough. Write down the name of the enemy and leave it with the flowers— that is, on the lid of Saint Erkenwald's tomb, where we'd received the third puzzle.

"It's a trap," Tom insisted. "'Come alone'? If this is

really from the Templars, why would they ask you who the enemy is? They already know the enemy."

"I think it's a test," I said. "Did I learn anything from what they gave me? Am I worthy to continue?"

"It even *smells* like a trap."

He wasn't wrong. And yet . . . "They went to all this trouble," I said, "helped us save the king, for what? To set a trap for *me*? They could have done that ages ago."

"It's still not smart," Sally said. "Please, Christopher."

I wished I could make them understand. It wasn't like I wanted to go alone. I didn't want to go at all. But if I hadn't followed the trail yesterday, the king—and many, many more people at the party—would have died.

"How about this?" I said. "Sally tells Lords Walsingham and Ashcombe what's happened. Tom goes with me to Saint Paul's, but I go into the church alone. I'll have my pistols; I'll keep my back to the wall. If anyone attacks me, I'll fire a shot to tell you to come in."

Tom began to protest that wasn't good enough, but I cut him off.

"I *have* to go, Tom," I said. "You know I do. His Majesty gave me to the spymaster. It's my job." Even if I'd never asked for it.

And with this, Tom quieted. He knew: We were apprentices. Our entire lives belonged to someone else. That sad look returned, the one I'd seen yesterday, after he'd been with Lord Ashcombe.

It's hard to say no to a king.

What on earth did they want him to do? I'd never found the right time to ask. And now I was wondering if it was too late.

But in the end, he agreed.

What choice did we have?

It was just an ordinary night.

That's what I kept telling myself as we rode in silence to Saint Paul's. People were out as usual, fewer than in full daylight, but enough to know the city was still alive.

I'd left Bridget with Sally, who'd shut the bird in my room before running off in search of Walsingham and Ashcombe. No doubt they were deep in preparations to leave. When we collected Blossom and Lightning from the stables, we saw the king's horses being hooked up to his carriage, everything getting ready to move His Majesty to Hampton Court. Whatever the Templars had to tell me, if it was a warning about the king, I hoped it would come quick.

We approached Saint Paul's through Ludgate, from the west. As agreed, Tom waited in the street. I handed him Blossom's reins and patted her neck. She nuzzled me, and my stomach tumbled. Something about that felt like a goodbye.

You're being ridiculous, I told myself. But that didn't quiet the fluttering in my gut.

The cathedral was lit now by candles. People mulled about in Paul's Walk, fewer than yesterday, but not by much. I skirted the crowd, scanning the faces as I passed. As promised, I kept my back to the wall, hands on the grips of my pistols.

Nothing seemed out of the ordinary. Again I told myself to stop being silly and went around the chancel to Saint Erkenwald's tomb. The flowers I'd placed there yesterday were gone. A few new offerings had been made today: a pouch knotted with string, a daffodil, and a simple ceramic cup. I placed the folded paper I was carrying on the lid, then backed away.

I'd barely stepped into the shadows when a girl my age, hair in long, blond braids and dressed in a simple peasant smock, approached from the chapel of Saint George in the northeast corner of the church. She reached over the rail and plucked the paper I'd left from the tomb. For all Tom's worry yesterday about stealing from a saint, no one even noticed she'd done it.

She unfolded the paper, read what I'd written inside. It was just a single word.

Covenanters.

She studied it for a moment. Then she tucked the paper inside her dress.

And turned to look directly at me.

CHAPTER
40

I FROZE.

Pressed against the wall, I tightened my grip on my pistols. For a moment, the girl didn't move. She just regarded me calmly.

Then she strode away.

She walked toward the north end of the cathedral. Before she disappeared, she stopped and looked back at me.

I hadn't moved. But as I stared at her, I finally understood what she wanted me to do.

I was supposed to follow.

I glanced around. No one seemed to be paying attention to either of us. If there was a threat somewhere, I couldn't see it.

I decided to chance it. Hands still on my pistols, I pushed myself from the wall.

The girl moved again, disappearing around the corner.

I hurried after her. When I caught sight of her, she was well ahead of me, moving deftly through the crowd. I thought she'd go out the main entrance, to the west, but instead, she took a side entrance, heading out of the cathedral to the north.

I hesitated. I'd left Tom watching the main entrance. If I followed the girl, he wouldn't know I'd gone.

I thought about firing a shot to alert him, but alert him to what? The girl wasn't threatening me. If anything, my shot was likely to scare her off. To say nothing of the fury it would cause in the church.

I stood there, not knowing what to do, until the girl decided for me. She'd stopped in the doorway, waiting. When I didn't move, she simply pushed the door open and left.

I followed her outside.

By the time I emerged, she was already across the courtyard. She'd bought a wax taper from one of the tallow boys outside the cathedral; the weak flame of the candle lit her way.

I hurried to follow, some thirty yards behind. She picked up the pace, moving northeast toward the junction of Newgate and Cheapside. I went after her, knowing Tom would be furious with me for leaving him behind. I could only hope I hadn't just made a terrible mistake.

She darted through the traffic, heading north. On Foster Lane, she stopped. She turned around, locked eyes with me once more.

Then she stepped into the shadows of an alley.

A clear invitation. But to what?

Go get Tom, I told myself.

I stood there, hesitant once more.

Go get Tom.

I wanted to. But if I left now, by the time I came back, I knew whatever waited for me in the alley would be gone. I'd already trusted the Templars this far.

You don't know it's the Templars, Master Benedict said.

No, I didn't. But when it came down to it, I had no more choice now than I'd had back at Whitehall. Whatever awaited, I was on my own.

I drew my pistols and followed her into the alley.

CHAPTER
41

IT WAS DARK.

The lights of travelers on the street couldn't reach into the cramped and narrow space between the houses. I waited a moment, a few feet into the shadows, to let my eyes adjust. To let my heart slow, get it to stop hammering in my chest.

I shifted my grip on the pistols. The wood was slippery, slick with sweat. I wiped my hands, took hold of the guns again. Then, cautious, I stepped forward.

The roofs blocked all but a faint band of stars. I could feel, more than see, the walls next to me. I used that sense and the starry road above to guide my way.

The alley turned left, first gradually, then sharply.

And then suddenly I saw a glow.

The girl was up ahead. Past private gardens to my right and left, the girl stood in a narrow intersection, where the alley crossed another. She was facing me, holding a lantern. She hadn't had a lantern before.

I stepped forward, intending to call to her. Before I could say a word, she turned to her right. The light faded, her silhouette dancing a mad shadow on the wall as she ran.

I moved faster now, pistols held tight, barrels forward and ready. At the intersection, I turned to follow—and found the alley had gone completely black. Her light had disappeared.

Then a new light flared, right in front of me. And I gasped.

It was an angel.

Not real, my mind said in rebellion. And of course that was true. It was just a man.

But he *looked* like an angel. His face was painted gold, his hair the same color. He was dressed in samite, the long robe shimmering in the flame of the lantern he'd ignited. His hands were almost like claws—not the gnarled, calloused claws of an animal, but smooth and graceful, his nails pointed like needles. And, sprouting from his back, were broad, feathered wings.

I barely had time to take this in when a second lantern flared to my right. Here stood another man, but this was no angel. He was a devil.

Not quite, my mind said, and of course he wasn't, either. But in my heart he was a devil. He wore a long, waxed-leather robe above buckled shoes. He had on thick gloves that looked almost like talons. In his left hand he held a lantern; in his right was a long, silver rod. Atop his head was a wide-brimmed hat. And his mask, his mask. Goggle eyes and a curved bird's beak.

A plague doctor. He was wearing a plague doctor's costume.

I barely had time to feel the terror before a new light came. Once more to my right, down the third alley. I looked.

And I beheld a knight.

A warrior of old, with dark eyes and a black beard, his head covered by a mail coif. He wore chain mail all over, in fact, except for his boots, which were solid but simple leather. He held a sword in one hand and a lantern in the other. The light illuminated his tabard, which hung to his knees. It was white, with a big red cross in the center.

A Templar, I thought, amazed.

And then a fourth lantern burned, lighting up my last

avenue of escape. I turned, and this time I saw a lady.

She was dressed all in white. White silk dress, white buckled shoes, white gloves, white hat, white parasol. Even her face was white, painted with thick makeup. The final figure to surround me, the memory of the ghost of Devonshire.

The White Lady.

They were all here. All my history, since Master Benedict had been killed.

The Cult of the Archangel.

The Plague Doctor.

The Templar.

And the Wraith.

I said nothing. My lips were frozen by confusion and fear. So it was the angel who spoke first, voice high and smooth.

"Do you have a coin?" he said.

I blinked. Were they going to *rob* me?

No, that didn't make sense. I stood there, dumb, until the plague doctor spoke, his voice muffled by his mask.

"Do you have a coin?"

I didn't understand. "I . . . I have some money with me—"

I whirled again, as a new voice spoke. Low and rumbling, like distant thunder. The knight.

"Do you have a coin?"

And it was as I stared at him, this knight of old

(not really, not really, he's just a man)

wearing a tabard not seen in centuries, that flared Templar cross, that it came to me. And I finally understood what they were asking.

"Yes," I said. "I have a coin."

"Show us," the White Lady said.

I tucked my pistols back in my belt. Then I reached, not into my coin purse, but to where I kept a secret, hidden deep in one of the pockets of my apothecary sash. My fingers found the metal, and I pulled it out.

It shone in the light of the four lanterns, bright, glittering gold. On one face was a flared cross, the twin of the symbol on the knight's tabard. *Baldvinus Rex de Ierusalem*, the coin read. King Baldwin of Jerusalem, first patron of the Knights Templar. I held the Templar florin up so she could see. So they all could see.

The knight's chain mail jingled as he held out his hand. In it was a letter, sealed with a simple circle of wax.

I took it from him. "Thank you," I said.

"You must hurry," he said. "Time is running out."

He put his lantern on the ground. The others did the same. Then they turned and walked off into the darkness.

Only I remained, blazing in the light.

CHAPTER
42

I RAN AS FAST AS I COULD.

Dodging through carriages, I sprinted across Cheapside, all the way back to Saint Paul's. I didn't go into the church. Instead, I skirted the cathedral, running through the yard to the end of Ludgate Street.

Tom wasn't there.

Where had he gone? I looked around but couldn't see him.

Had someone made off with him?

No, I thought. He was a giant with a massive sword and an old warhorse. Who'd be so stupid as to attack Tom? He'd probably gone looking for me. I'd been away a lot longer than expected.

That meant he'd be in the church. I ran toward the entrance, and sure enough, there was Blossom, with Lightning, both held by a boy near a hitching post, charging a farthing a horse. I ran to him.

"Where'd the boy who gave you these horses go?" I said, but he didn't need to answer.

"Christopher!" Tom bounded down the steps of the church, face red—relieved, and a little angry. "Where on earth have you been? I looked for you all over—"

"I met them," I said.

"Met who? What are you . . . ?"

His eyes widened. *The Templars?* he mouthed.

I nodded. "They gave me a new message."

I held up the letter. The boy with the horses looked from Tom to me, confused, wondering what we were on about.

"What does it say?" Tom said.

"That we have to get back to the palace."

We rode hard into the stables at Scotland Yard. Tom slid from his saddle and began to lead Lightning automatically toward his stall. Normally, I'd have done the same with Blossom, to brush our horses down and give them water. But we didn't have time for that.

"Let the groom handle them," I said. "We have to get to—"

"Christopher!"

"Ho! What are you doing there!"

The two voices came at me at once. The first was Sally. Waiting across the courtyard, she'd spotted our arrival and was now running to join us. The second was the groom.

He jogged up to me, angry. "I said, what are you doing?" He grabbed the reins from my hand and shoved me away.

I stumbled, nearly tripping in the mud before righting myself. Blossom snorted, ears twitching. I stared back at the man, confused. "What's the matter?"

Tom looked just as startled as the groom grabbed Lightning's reins, too. Though he didn't try to push Tom.

"Who gave you permission to take these horses?" the man said.

I didn't recognize him; he hadn't been here the previous times we'd visited the stables. But none of the grooms had challenged us before. Was it because he hadn't seen us come from the palace? Or had something else gone wrong at Whitehall?

"Lord Ashcombe said we could use them," I explained.

"Is that so? And I suppose King Charles tucks you into bed each night?"

My blood grew hot, and I made to retort before Tom put a calming hand on my arm. I clamped my mouth shut.

"That's right," the groom said. "Now clear out of my yard."

Tom led me away before I said anything I might regret. "It's not worth the trouble," he said.

"We didn't do anything wrong," I said hotly, but Tom was right. We had much more important things to worry about.

Sally joined us, puzzled. "What was all that about?"

"Someone self-important, throwing his weight around," I said, and not quietly.

Firmly, Tom pushed me farther from the stalls. "Did you find Lords Walsingham and Ashcombe?"

"Walsingham's at Guildhall," Sally said. Guildhall was the seat of London's government, where the offices for the Lord Mayor and the magistrates were. "And Lord Ashcombe left with His Majesty."

"They're gone?" I said, not sure if I should be relieved or dismayed.

"Just after you two went to Saint Paul's. Why? What's happened?"

"The king's still in danger."

I told her about meeting the Templars and pulled the new letter from beneath my waistcoat. The seal was broken; I'd scanned the letter before hurrying back to Tom. Now I handed it over for them to read.

So the final act is played,
The final truth decrypted,

Still your master dies betrayed—
For every scene was scripted.

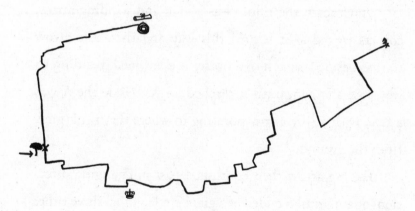

"'The final act,'" Sally read, "and final truth. And . . . 'your master dies betrayed'?"

"Do they mean Lord Walsingham?" Tom said.

"I think they're talking about His Majesty," I said. "I may be apprenticed to the spymaster, but our ultimate master is the king. And that's who these plots are against."

It was the only thing that made sense. Poisoning the party wouldn't have killed Lord Walsingham; he was never going. And then there was the second line of the riddle.

Still your master dies betrayed.

In other words: Everything we'd done to protect the king was still going to fail. I shook my head. The spymaster had been right; this wasn't over.

Sally studied the diagram on the paper. "What's this, then?"

Underneath the riddle was a long and winding arrow, corners jagged as it turned this way and that. The arrow started beside a sketch of a horse. It continued, bending its way past a crown, until it reached an *X*. Beside the *X* was a tree, with a tiny arrow pointing to where the trunk grew from the ground.

The big arrow then continued past it, changing directions again, until it ended at a giant circle, inked three times around. Beside the circle was the drawing of a scroll, rolled up and tied with ribbon.

"Looks like a treasure map," Tom said.

I thought so, too. But I doubted the end held any treasure. "A path to follow, maybe?"

"To the king?" Sally suggested. "That's what the crown could mean."

There was logic in that. I followed the arrow. "If up is north, then maybe it means . . . the king rides from Whitehall? If that's what this horse is? He goes southwest . . . and that *is* the direction of Hampton Court. So is this arrow supposed to be the road?"

"Does the road bend like that?"

I didn't think so.

"If it is the king's route," Tom said, "why does it go *past* the crown? There's an *X* over here, by the tree, but there's nothing where the crown is."

"Maybe that's supposed to indicate the king is going that way, not that he's there." Though that didn't seem right to me.

"I don't understand how anyone's supposed to follow all these twists and turns anyway," Tom said. "This looks like a path through a maze. But without the maze."

A maze? I thought.

My mind began to race.

A maze, Master Benedict said, and nodded.

That was it.

CHAPTER
43

"YOU'VE DONE IT." I GRABBED TOM'S arm and shook him. "You've done it *again*."

"Naturally," he said proudly. "Er . . . what did I do?"

"This diagram. It *is* for a maze."

"Which one?" Sally said.

"The same one we've been complaining about since we got here." I reached under my apothecary sash and pulled out the map that Dobson, the old servant, had given us. "It's Whitehall. The arrow is a path through the palace."

"Look," I said. "Over here, on the right side, is where we are now. The stables. And look at the letter—there's a drawing of a horse. If you follow the arrow . . ." I traced a route along the map. "Remember what Dobson said? The numbers on the map show who's lodged where. Number *1* belongs to the king—and that's where the crown is."

Tom peered at it. "It does look like that."

"It is. In fact—come on." I rushed over to where a torch was burning in a sconce on the wall. Carefully, I laid the page with the arrow on top of the map. Then I held the whole thing up to the flame.

The light shone a soft orange through the pages. Held this way, the ink was visible on both of them.

And the arrow traced a route through the palace exactly.

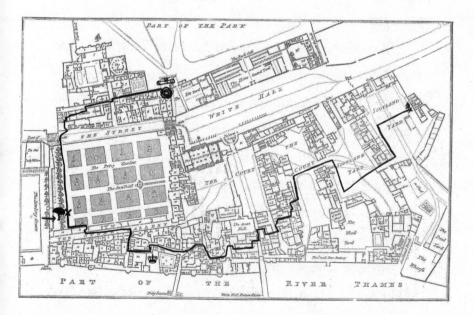

"That's it," Sally said, amazed. "The horse is right on the stables . . . the crown is on the king's rooms."

"So we follow it, then?" Tom said.

"We do," I said. "And see what we find."

It was a long and convoluted route. I had a mind to simply run to where the tree was marked, but I thought there might be something to see along the way. So we hurried, as fast as we dared, while still keeping our eyes peeled.

We started where the arrow started, back at the stables. When the groom spotted us again, he stormed toward us, fists clenched. We got out of there soon enough.

From the stables, we crossed Scotland Yard, then into the Court. From there, it was a path through the pastry and the kitchen and around the buttery, before entering the heart of the palace via the chapel. We passed close to our quarters; then a zigzag path through the corridors led us straight past the king's section of the palace.

"This is the first time," Tom said, "we actually know where we're going."

No one stopped us; we'd been seen enough around Whitehall the past few days that our faces were familiar.

We watched carefully the whole time, but seeing nothing out of the ordinary, we moved on.

The arrow directed us outside, through the Stone Gallery, and suddenly we were in the Privy Garden. We skirted the garden itself, heading south until we reached the apple trees that lined the edge of the grass.

"Which tree should we look at?" Sally said.

The *X* had been marked over the third tree up, but there were more here than the map showed. "Let's start at the third from the end, and go from there."

"What are we looking for?" Tom said.

"I don't know. Maybe an actual *X*?"

"The little arrow is aimed at the ground," Sally noted.

"So let's look there, too. Maybe what we're trying to find is buried. Check to see if the earth has been disturbed."

There wasn't enough light to see in the orchard; we had to run back inside to get lanterns. Then we began to search. Sally checked the bark for marks. Tom and I inspected the soil around the trunks. He reached the fifth tree before he called to me. "Christopher."

I went over. He knelt on the grass in front of a darker spot on the ground. The earth here had been turned over recently, then patted down.

Tom was already digging his fingers into the dirt. He rooted around for a moment, then stopped. "There's something. . . ."

He pulled out a little object wrapped in cloth. He shook the soil off, then unfolded the wrapping. Metal glinted in the flame.

It was a key.

"What does it open?" Sally said.

"I'm guessing whatever we find at the end of the arrow," I said. "Let's go."

CHAPTER
44

WE WENT FASTER THIS TIME. THE arrow led us past Westminster Gate, over the tennis courts, then back into more apartments, until we reached the room where the arrow ended. It was beside the old tilt-yard, where knights had jousted in the days of Elizabeth and Henry VIII.

On the map, this room was circled. It was one of three rooms listed with the number *33*. The door was closed.

"What now?" Tom whispered.

He and Sally kept watch as I knocked at the door, softly. When no one answered, I tried the knob.

Locked.

I remembered what Lord Ashcombe had said. *Nothing is locked in the palace.*

Fingers trembling, I inserted the key we'd found buried by the tree in the Privy Garden. It turned smoothly.

Clack.

I stood there, hand on the knob, but I didn't open it. "Just a second," I said to the others.

"Where are you going?" Sally said.

I hurried back through the corridor, catching up to a pair of servants we'd passed along the way. "Excuse me?"

I showed them my map, keeping the message with the long arrow hidden. I pointed to the quarters marked *33.* "Could you tell me whose rooms are these?"

"Colonel Darcy's, sir," the older servant said.

I had no idea who that was. But I thought it might look suspicious to ask, so I just said, "Thank you," and turned to go.

"You won't find him there, however," the man said. "The colonel is in Cambridge for another two weeks."

"Oh." I decided to chance it. "Is someone staying there instead?"

"Yes, sir. Colonel Darcy was gracious enough to permit the Baron of Oxton to stay at Whitehall while the colonel is away."

The Baron of Oxton.

Domhnall Ardrey.

The man I'd seen outside the palace gates. The man who'd appeared in the Banqueting House.

I thanked the servants and hurried back.

We went inside.

I left the door unlocked, in case we needed to make a quick escape. We found ourselves in a sitting room, a bedroom to the left. The rooms were dark; I took one of the blankets from the bed, to stuff at the bottom of the door so no one passing would see the light from our lanterns.

"What are we looking for?" Tom whispered.

The Templars' map showed a scroll of paper. "A letter," I whispered back. "Or something like it."

That was just a guess, but it gave us a place to start. And we needed to hurry. We had no idea where Lord Ardrey was. He might come back at any time.

Tom and I began at the desk, shuffling through the papers atop it, before opening the drawers. Sally took the bedroom.

Nothing in the papers seemed of interest. Most looked to be documents for a land deal near the baron's estate in

Scotland; if that was a threat to the king, I couldn't see how. The rest was private correspondence, mostly gossip.

Sally joined us in the sitting room. "Anything?" I said, and she shook her head.

Tom glanced nervously at the door. "What now?"

This couldn't be it. The Templars' letter had led us here; there had to be something to find. "Check everywhere. Hiding spots. Secret compartments. Anywhere you can think."

Sally returned to the bedroom to give it another look. Tom checked the couch. I stayed with the desk, knocking at the wood, prying the panels to see if anything popped out. Eventually, frustrated, I yanked out the drawers and dumped them on the floor.

Nothing. Nothing hidden, nothing underneath. I crawled under the desk—

And there it was.

Tucked under the wood, right at the back. By pulling the drawers out, I'd exposed a secret panel. Pressing the front of it made the panel pop open, and a letter, folded tightly, fell to the rug.

I grabbed it and crawled out from under the desk. Sally, who'd heard the commotion, hurried from the bedroom to find me sitting at Tom's feet, holding the letter.

I opened it, and we all read it together.

D.—

Your plan has worked. The enemy and their agent were deceived. The man in black informed me secretly that the threat inside the palace has forced the oath breaker out. He will be taken tonight by carriage to Hampton Court.

Tell F. to camp his men at the bend by the river, hidden in Barnham Wood; it's the best site for an ambush. All must answer the call—there will be a score in the escort, at least. God willing, we shall finally hold the oath breaker to account. The Lord our righteousness!

—N.

My guts twisted.

Tom was confused. "What is all this?"

Your plan worked, the letter said.

"The oath breaker," I said, voice quavering, "is the

king. The threat inside the palace . . . the murders . . . the poison . . . The whole point of them was to force His Majesty to leave Whitehall.

"And the Covenanters . . . they're waiting. There's going to be an ambush."

Your plan worked.

For every scene was scripted.

The Covenanters had planned this all along. Their enemy—the Knights Templar—and their agent . . . that was me. We'd been used.

I'd been used.

And now the king was riding to his death.

What had I done?

CHAPTER
45

I BOLTED FROM THE ROOM.

Tom and Sally shouted after me. "Christopher! Wait!"

I couldn't wait. This was my fault. *My* fault.

I rushed from the west wing, sprinted across the tilt-yard. Into the street—

"LOOK OUT!"

The hackney driver pulled hard on the reins. His horses squealed, carriage wheels juddering in the dirt. I heard the axle crack, and the carriage lurched sideways, nearly throwing the driver from his seat.

"You stupid—!" A string of curses followed, enough to strip paint from walls. I didn't stop.

My fault.

Down the street, into Scotland Yard. The stables.

"Blossom!" I called. "Blossom!"

She neighed in response. Her head poked from her stall, ears pricked forward, alert. I reached for the latch—

And then a man tackled me from behind.

My head jerked, slamming into the man's shoulder. I fell, the weight of him on top of me, landing facedown in the dirt. I'd been reaching out when I was tackled, and a good thing, too, because if he'd pinned my arms to my chest, I wouldn't have had my hands to break the fall.

As it was, the ground was soft, muddied by a light rain earlier in the day. I got a bit of wind knocked out, but it didn't feel like anything was broken.

I tried to wriggle out from underneath. A forearm smashed my face back into the mud. I tasted earth and grit.

Above me, Blossom snorted in fear. The stall rattled as a hoof smashed into it.

"Got you now," a voice growled in my ear.

My mind, shaken from the fall, shaken even more by the Scotsman's letter, was confused. For a moment, I thought Tom had tackled me to stop me running away. But of course Tom wouldn't hurt me—

The groom. He lay on top of me, pressing down with cruel delight. He leaned in and whispered gleefully in my ear. "Little thief. I can kill you now. It's my *right*."

He never got the chance. One second, I was pinned in the mud, the next, I was rising, dragged up by his arms. Then, suddenly, he let go, and I was facedown in the dirt again.

The groom yelled in alarm. I rolled over just in time to see what happened.

Tom had arrived. He'd pulled the man off me—literally picked him up. He lifted the groom overhead. Then he slammed him to the ground like a bale of hay.

A knife flew from the groom's hands, skittered through the mud. *He really was going to kill me,* I thought, dazed. *Why does he hate me so—?*

And then I understood.

"Hold him," I croaked to Tom.

Tom looked at me, confused. "Why was he—?"

"Hold him!"

The groom, stunned and clumsy, tried to rise. Tom grabbed the man's arms, twisted them back, and mashed him face-first into the earth.

"Let me go!" the groom shouted.

Sally reached us. She covered her mouth in shock,

then hurried to help me up. "What happened?"

I spat dirt from my teeth. "He's one of them."

"I am not!" the groom's voice carried across the yard. "I'm loyal to the king!"

Tom's throw must have rattled the man's brain. Or maybe he just wasn't that bright to begin with. Either way, he'd made a mistake.

"If you're not one of them," I said, "then how do you know what I'm talking about?"

The man sputtered, then stopped. Tom held him fast. There was little point in keeping up the pretense now.

He sneered at me. "You're too late, unfaithful. Your heretic king dies tonight. The Lord our righteousness!"

The Lord our righteousness. The same as in the letter.

The Covenanters' battle cry.

"What do we do with him?" Tom said.

I rose, stiffly, and unlatched the door to Blossom's stall. She stomped out nervously. I patted her neck, trying to calm her, while reaching for the saddle hanging inside.

"Take him to the guard and have him locked up as a Covenanter," I said. Sally helped me strap on my saddle. "Then follow me as soon as you can."

"Follow you?" Tom said. "You can't go alone. Just

wait for me!"

"I can't! I can't wait! They're going to ambush the king! I have to warn him! Just don't let *him* go. There's no telling what problems he'll cause."

"What can I do?" Sally said.

"Grab all the guards the palace can spare. Have them follow us."

But there was a problem.

"The guards have already gone," she said, "with Lord Ashcombe and the king. There'll only be a few left."

I cursed. No matter how many soldiers were with Charles, if they walked into an ambush . . .

Suddenly it came to me. "Berkshire House!"

"What about it?"

"The party," I said. "Lord Walsingham said he'd make it look as if the king was coming. There'll be soldiers all over the grounds."

Sally was already running. "Send them after us, quick as they can!" I shouted as I climbed into the saddle.

Tom dragged the groom through the dirt. "Just wait one minute!" he called to me.

I couldn't. There was no time.

I rode off into the street.

CHAPTER 46

BLOSSOM'S HOOVES THUNDERED
in the mud.

My fault, I thought. *It's my fault.*

The horse galloped through the darkness. Ignoring the
protests of the guard on duty, I'd snatched a torch from
Holbein Gate on the way south. It was the only thing lighting our way.

My fault.

My body rattled with every stride. I'd never ridden this
fast. I tried to do as Lord Ashcombe had taught me. *Lift
your seat from the saddle. Crouch over it. Let your feet support
your weight in the stirrups.*

It worked, at least for a while. My knees, bent, dampened the shock of Blossom's gallop, like bow springs on a carriage. But I had miles to go, and my legs weren't strong enough to carry my weight the whole way. Eventually, I fell into the saddle and just took the punishment. It was no less than I deserved.

That's enough, child, Master Benedict said gently.

It's not, I said. *It'll never be enough. It's my fault.*

You're being unkind. The fault lies where it always lies: in the hearts of the wicked, who do wicked things. You know this.

Even so. They used me.

So they did. Now it's up to you to undo it. Focus on the problem. Clear your mind and focus.

I closed my eyes, let Blossom guide us down the road. The cleverness of the Covenanters, their deviousness, was almost impossible to believe. It had even fooled the Templars.

So the final act is played,
The final truth decrypted,

Still your master dies betrayed—
For every scene was scripted.

Everything had started with the murders of the servants at the palace. There'd never been any clear reason to kill them. I'd thought the girls had seen things they shouldn't have, but now I wondered: What if they hadn't seen anything at all? *What if the only purpose of the murders was to show the king there was a threat inside the palace?*

It had certainly worked. The palace got locked down. Security was increased. We realized there were traitors inside. Just no one knew who they were.

Once we'd made Whitehall more secure, the Covenanters had—seemingly—moved their plot to Berkshire House. It was no secret the king would be attending a party. If they poisoned the food, maybe they could kill His Majesty there.

But that plot, too, had been exposed—by me, with the aid of the Templars.

Traitors in Whitehall, traitors in Berkshire House. The walls were closing in. It was clear that nowhere was safe.

The smart thing to do would be to move Charles somewhere the Covenanters hadn't already infiltrated. Get him out of the palace. So that's what we'd done.

But what was it Lord Ashcombe had said? *They can't attack the palace directly. It would be suicide.*

But if they could get the king *out* of Whitehall . . .
outside the protection of its walls . . .

And if they knew *when* the king would be leaving, and where he was going . . .

I shuddered as I remembered what Lord Ardrey's letter had said.

Your plan has worked. The enemy and their agent were deceived.

They couldn't get to Charles inside the palace. So they'd maneuvered us to move the king *outside.* Where the Covenanter soldiers *could* attack him.

We'd thought we were leading the king to safety. Instead, we'd sent him into an ambush.

And the Covenanters had used me to help them do it.

I despaired. We'd fallen into their trap. Even the Templars hadn't realized it, until the end. How could the Covenanters be so clever?

And as I sank in despair, I recalled one more thing in Ardrey's letter. I could barely bear to remember it.

The man in black informed me, it said.

Walsingham had told me the plan to move the king wouldn't remain a secret. Even so, there couldn't have been that many who knew what was happening. And I'd only ever seen one man in black. One man who *always* wore black.

Lord Ashcombe.

The King's Warden.

A Covenanter?

A *traitor*?

My mind rebelled at the thought. It couldn't be. It just couldn't.

But if he was . . .

Blossom's stride changed underneath me.

The terrible thoughts in my head faded as my horse began to slow. Lost in my own mind, I hadn't been paying attention to her.

She was tiring. Great breaths blew from her nostrils, puffing mist in the cool air. We must have covered several miles already, going hard, and she wasn't built for this. She was a carriage horse, slow but steady, and now she was old.

Fear wrenched at my gut. Sally had said the king left an hour before Tom and I returned to Whitehall. Add another twenty or so minutes to follow the trail of the Templars' map and find the letter in Lord Ardrey's room . . . That meant they had nearly an hour-and-a-half head start. My only salvation

CHAPTER
47

I SLAMMED INTO THE GROUND.

Pain ripped through my body as I hit the dirt. My momentum carried me forward, and what started as a skid turned into a roll. I lost my torch, the flame tumbling in my vision, until it was just a glow in the distance. Then I finally came to a stop.

I was on my back. The stars spun above me, swirling, then resetting their place and doing it all over again. My stomach twisted, but I was too dazed to heave.

What had happened?

For a second, I thought I'd broken everything. Because everything hurt. Then the pain faded, at least a little, was that the king was in a carriage, which moved slower if everyone was on horseback. Riding Blossom, I had a chance to catch them. If I had to stop . . .

I leaned forward, a hand on her withers. "Come Blossom," I said, and her ears turned back to me. "Pl keep going. I need you."

She seemed to understand. Her pace quickened, ho thundering on the road once more. I patted her neck. "G girl," I said.

Then she squealed, a terrible cry of pain.

And I was flying.

enough that I could move. Once again, I tasted dirt, now mixed with the metallic tang of blood.

My face was wet. I brought an aching arm to my lip, and it came away warm. I was bleeding.

I turned my head, trying to get my bearings. I was lying on the road, that much I knew, but I couldn't tell which way was forward and which was back. I tried to sit up. Dazed, I fell, to look once more at swirling stars.

Get up, Master Benedict said.

I managed to prop myself on my elbows. Why did everything have to spin so?

And . . . what had happened?

Blossom squealed, in pain and fear. I looked down the road and saw her struggling to rise, my torch near her feet. There was something in the dirt. Twisted, nearly the color of the earth. It looked like . . . a snake?

No. It was too long. One end, near Blossom, was fastened to a wooden stake. The other end was tied to a second stake pulled nearly horizontal—

A rope. That's what it was.

Someone had strung a rope across the road.

I'd barely realized this when a flash lit the meadow and a boom rocked the dark. A puff of dirt kicked up, two feet to my right. And I recognized that sound right away.

Someone was shooting at me.

Now I moved. I scrambled forward, crawling headfirst into the ditch beside the highway. It was dark down here, the road between me and whoever had just taken that shot. Blossom, finally on her feet, whinnied and reared, forelegs kicking in fright. She stamped about, eyes rolling, running in a circle.

What was she doing? Was she looking for me?

Run, I thought. She was too easy a target. *Run!*

A second shot came from the meadow. It smashed through the pommel on my saddle, scattering shreds of leather in the mud. Blossom squealed and bolted into the dark.

I was relieved to see her go. But now I was alone. I just sat there, crouched in the ditch, for what felt like forever, the only sounds my breath, and the *whump whump whump* of my heart.

My pistols, I thought. I reached for them and found only one. The second must have tumbled from my belt when I fell.

I drew the one I had, gripped it, my palm slick. *Master, what do I do?*

Keep your head, he said. *And move.*

Right. Whoever was shooting at me couldn't see me in the ditch. He'd have no idea where I was. I shifted, crawling a good thirty yards before I dared to take a peek.

The road was lit by my torch, burning faintly as it lay in the dirt. I couldn't see much past—

Another shot came, the bullet whistling overhead. I saw the muzzle of their gun flash in the meadow. Reflexively, I fired back. My flintlock fizzed, then boomed in my hand, kicking into my palm, before I dived back into the ditch.

I doubted I'd hit anything. My hands were shaking. And from the muzzle flash, my enemy had to be fifty yards away. The original shot had come from much closer, that first burst fifteen yards from the edge. The shooter must have retreated.

And it was *a* shooter, a single man; I was sure of it. There was too much time between shots, just enough for one man to reload his musket.

They left a separate ambush, in case someone followed? I reloaded my own pistol with the powder in my apothecary sash, thinking, *Does that mean I'm close?*

I listened. The night was still, just my breath and my heart. No answering gunfire, no horn blaring an alarm.

Hope faded as I realized however close I was to the king, I wasn't close enough.

And yet . . . sound carried, especially on a chilly night like this. I peeked over the ridge of the road, and as the muzzle flashed at me from across the meadow, I fired in return. The enemy's bullet hit the mud; I didn't know about mine. Again I reloaded, waiting.

Still there was nothing.

Despair returned. Poor Blossom, terrified and in pain, had bolted somewhere into the night. While I was grateful for that—if she'd stayed, she'd be dead, lost to a Covenanter's bullet—I now realized that I was stuck. Even if I could chase my ambusher off, I had no way of catching up to the king's company. Maybe if Sally managed to find more soldiers . . . but it would take time to round them up. Only Tom—

Tom! I thought desperately. *He'll follow sooner. And if he doesn't realize there's a Covenanter in the meadow . . .*

Surely he'd hear the shots and stop?

Or would he come more quickly, thinking I was in danger?

I had to warn him. And I had to warn the king.

But how? If our shots hadn't done the job, what else did I have?

The image came then, so clearly. Master Benedict raised an eyebrow and said, *What else do you have, indeed?*

And I understood.

I fumbled about under my shirt. My apothecary sash. It didn't only hold reloads for my pistol. I still had two—

There.

My fireworks.

They were four inches long and cylindrical, with a three-inch tail of cannon fuse at one end. The paper-cone noses had been crushed—so had the cylinders, a bit—but I could mend that.

I took the map of Whitehall from my coat and tore it in half. Each piece I curled into a cone and fixed to the top of the fireworks with birch gum from one of the vials in my sash. I hoped the gum would keep them stuck on. I didn't have time to cure it.

A shot whizzed overhead. The sound made me flinch, even though I knew he couldn't hit me in the ditch. *He's feeling me out,* I thought.

Well, he was in for a surprise. Now that the nose cones were stuck to my fireworks, I needed a stick to serve as a launcher. I cursed. I couldn't see one in the ditch, and with the Covenanter out there shooting at shadows,

I didn't dare go crawling to find one. What was I to do—

Of course.

My pistol.

It wasn't ideal—I'd probably burn my hand a bit—but what choice did I have? I dumped the gunpowder from the frizzen, then tied the first of the fireworks to the end. Then I lit the fuse, pointed the pistol at the sky, and waited, eyes closed.

I did burn my skin. But it only stung a little as the firework shot upward, into the sky.

The paper cone came off about ten yards up, spiraling down onto the road. Unbalanced, the firework wobbled and flew in an erratic arc.

Then it exploded. There was a boom, a little too soft, and while the burst flared, it was only half of what it should have been. The cylinder must have lost powder along the way.

My heart sank. I had only one more chance. I double-wrapped this firework, using the Templars' final letter, and smeared all the gum I had on the cone until it wouldn't come off in my fingers. I smeared aloe on my hand, too, berating myself for not thinking of doing that the first time, to shield me from the burning powder.

A shot flew over the road. I ignored it. I held my pistol straight up, away from my face, and lit the fuse.

It flew. My firework rocketed away, burning so furiously that I was shocked. Until I remembered with joy that—just as an experiment, of course, and while Tom's back had been turned—I'd double-loaded a couple of the fireworks.

This one performed flawlessly. It flew so high that the flame out the back looked little more than a candle.

Then it exploded.

The BOOM echoed in my ears. Streams of silver light burst outward, a glorious display that lit up the night. I wondered what the Covenanter out there was thinking. I hoped it was nothing good, and wished him every evil in the world.

A cry came from up the road. "Christopher!"

"Tom!" I stared in horror at the lantern, rocking up and down in the distance as Tom approached, astride Lightning at full gallop. "Get down! Someone's out there!"

"What?"

He couldn't hear me over his horse. Desperately, I dumped powder into the frizzen of my pistol, the wood scorched and smoking, and stuck my head up over the ditch, aiming into the meadow.

The firework had lit the whole area like a flare. I saw a glint of metal where I'd seen the shooter earlier. His musket!

I nearly fired; I stopped my finger from pulling the trigger just in time. The musket was on the ground. The shooter had left it behind when he fled.

My fireworks had chased him away.

Tom slowed, pulling on the reins until Lightning came to a snorting stop, stamping his feet as he eyed the rope-snake in the road.

Tom looked horrified as, muddy and bleeding, I climbed from the ditch. "What happened?" he said.

"They set a trap," I said. "Blossom hit the rope—she fell. . . ."

Tom looked around, still confused, but there wasn't much to see anymore. My firework had burned out. The only light now came from Tom's lantern, my fallen torch, and the stars.

"Where is Blossom?"

I'd have liked to find her, see she was all right, but there was no time. We had to get to the king.

I found my other pistol; it was near where I'd first hit the ground. I stuffed it in my belt. Then I climbed up on Lightning, behind Tom. He kicked his heels, and we were off.

The old warhorse tore up the road. I held on to Tom, bleeding, aching, afraid I might fly off the back. And an image came to me then, as we'd seen it in Paris.

Two brothers on one horse, I thought.

A symbol of the Knights Templar. Was it an omen?

Then I heard the sounds of battle up ahead.

CHAPTER
48

IT WAS A SCENE OF HORROR.

The road stretched away, disappearing into the woods.

And that road was littered with bodies.

There had to be nearly forty of them, starting from the edge of the trees, over a span of seventy yards. The king's carriage, adorned with golden trim, lay overturned, its horses dead, still tied in the traces. My stomach dropped as my eyes fell on the wreckage, expecting to see the lifeless form of His Majesty

(my fault)

but he wasn't there.

More horses lay among the men, the scene cast in the

eerie glow of fallen, fluttering torches. There was enough light to see that most of the dead did *not* wear beige tabards with the king's coat of arms—they were not the King's Men. These were Covenanter dead.

The roar of battle came from our right. There the King's Men were making their stand, fighting atop a ridge to which they'd retreated. It was a good defensive position—at least, the best that could be found in the meadow. Around the ridge was a ditch, which acted like a natural, dry moat. It gave the King's Men the advantage of height, from which they could strike down at the surrounding Covenanters.

Around them was a ring of bodies: carcasses of the King's Men's horses, which, from the bullet wounds, had taken the brunt of the initial volley of gunfire from the ambushers, saving the men sheltered behind them. Now more bodies were being added to the ring, as the battle was fought, forming a mound the enemy needed to stumble over.

Lord Ashcombe stood side by side with his troops, holding the Covenanter mob at bay. The odds looked grim. Even though the King's Men were in a strong position, I counted less than twenty of them standing. There were four times as many Covenanters still alive.

Holding Lightning's reins one-handed, Tom drew Eternity from its sheath. The blade rang with holy song. Tom's arm was steady, even as his voice quavered.

"Hold on tight," he said, trembling.

Then he turned his horse directly into the fray.

Lightning's hooves churned the dirt as he reached his full speed. He roared, a challenge, as if remembering battles long fought and eager to relive them. I drew a pistol, my other hand clinging to Tom's waist.

A gap was forming in the circle of King's Men atop the ridge. Tom angled Lightning toward it, sword held ready. The Covenanters, focused on the surrounded Royalists, didn't see us coming until it was too late.

Eternity caught one of the enemy in the back. Three more men screamed as they were trampled, falling under Lightning's iron shoes.

One man turned to face us. I fired. I think I hit him, but I was never sure, because just then Lightning leaped across the ditch.

We sailed through the air.

Then we landed heavily atop the ridge. Tom yanked hard on the reins as the King's Men shifted to close the gap. A hand grabbed the bridle, bringing us to a halt inside the circle.

I looked down to see the hand belonged to Charles, our king. He held a sword, just a simple blade, retrieved from one of his fallen men. His eyes gleamed with fire—the flame of the torches and the blaze of battle.

"Didn't want to miss all the fun, eh?" he shouted with defiant glee as he helped us down from the warhorse.

Then our fight began in earnest.

CHAPTER

49

A KING'S MAN FELL RIGHT BESIDE
Lord Ashcombe. Tom took his place, hacking and slash-
ing with Eternity at the spears, halberds, and poleaxes that
thrust forward to open the gap. Men fell under his blade
as he used all that Sir William Leech, Captain Tanner,
and the King's Men had taught him, and so, too, his own
God-given strength.

I stayed with him, just behind, filled with terror. I
thought of picking up a blade—I eyed a fallen halberd,
wanting desperately to grab it and join him—but I knew
my skill was no match for the Covenanters. Instead, I helped
him how I could: with my pistols.

I timed my shots carefully. I placed one hand on Tom's back, the other holding a gun at the ready. Anytime a gap opened beside Tom, I fired. When a shoving halberd unbalanced him, I fired. When a spear gouged the side of his leg, and he stumbled, I reached over his shoulder and fired, giving Tom time to steady himself.

After every shot, I reloaded. It was automatic now. Dump the powder in. Jam the paper wadding in the barrel. Ram down the ball. Fill the frizzen. Wait till Tom needed me.

Then fire.

The battle battered my ears. The boom of my guns, the clash of blades, the screams of the dying. The war cries, too.

"The Lord our righteousness!" the Covenanters shouted—

"Havoc!" Lord Ashcombe howled in return. A command to destroy everything, it was the greatest defiance he could cast at them, even as the King's Men fell.

War now was my only thought, my only existence. Steel and smoke, blood and death. The bodies piled higher, making it harder for the Covenanters to get to us, but for every five of them, we lost one, and our circle got smaller.

Still I fought.

Fire. Powder, paper, ball.

Fire. Powder, paper, ball.

Fire.

And then I was out. My powder, my shot, all used up.

"I'm empty!" I shouted to Tom, warning him.

He nodded, focused on the enemy. But Lord Ashcombe, beside him, heard me. He ripped a pouch from his belt and threw it backward, where it hit me in the leg and fell to the ground. His own supply: powder horn and shot, for the pearl-handled pistols at his side.

I picked it up, reloaded.

Powder, paper, ball.

Fire.

There were only ten of the King's Men left now. Charles had joined the fray, on the other side of Lord Ashcombe. He was a skilled swordsman, a warrior in his own right from an age even younger than Tom and I were now, and he fought well. The Covenanters recognized him and howled in glee, finally seeing their prize within reach.

But as they focused on the king, they left themselves open, and Lord Ashcombe, Tom, and I took full advantage, taking them down so quickly they had to swing their attention our way once more.

Powder, paper, ball.

Fire.

But still they pressed, and still we fell. Numbers ten and nine of the King's Men went down in hard fighting. Eight, seven, and six just seemed to disappear, and we had to close in tight to fill the gaps. Five and four fell to Covenanter spears, and then there were only seven of us in total and more than twenty of them, and surely we were dead.

So . . . why were the Covenanters running?

All but four of them turned and fled. Their companions looked startled to be left alone all of a sudden, and the King's Men cut them down until there were none. The remaining score of Covenanters sprinted toward the woods.

Then, through the ringing in my ears, I heard the thunder of horses. And I saw, galloping down the road from London, a score of lanterns swinging in the dark.

King's Men, upon warhorses, rode into view, chasing the fleeing Covenanters to cut them down.

Sally had sent us reinforcements from Berkshire House.

How I adore that girl, I thought.

And then it was over.

We howled. No longer screams of pain or horror, but jubilation—sheer, unbridled joy. The battle was over.

And it was the most *real* thing I'd ever experienced.

The terror I'd felt had burrowed deeper than any before.

So, too, did the exhilaration when I realized that no, I wasn't going to die after all. I understood then, how soldiers spoke of the ecstasy of war, not just the fighting but the moment after, when you're still alive, victorious.

I hugged Tom, and the soldiers, and even Lord Ashcombe. The king, too, embraced us all, joining us as we thrust our weapons high and howled our defiance into the night. We'd held the circle. Held it long enough, just enough, so we got to live. It was the most extraordinary, most joyous thing I'd ever felt.

And I would pray, every night, until the end of my days, that I would never have to feel that way again.

CHAPTER
50

"ARE YOU ALL RIGHT?"

I heard the words, but their meaning didn't even register. It took a hand grabbing my shoulder and spinning me around to bring me back to earth.

"Well?" Lord Ashcombe said.

I was still in a bit of a daze, so he looked me over.

"You're wounded," he said.

I was?

I looked down to see my coat sliced open on the left, below my shoulder. It was stained with blood. When I took the coat off, I saw more blood, wet, and the gash in my shirt. Someone's blade had got past Tom and cut me.

"I don't even feel it," I said, amazed.

"Give it a minute. You will."

Lord Ashcombe himself had countless cuts and bruises, though none looked serious. Tom also had a few, the worst of which was the spear wound in his lower thigh, but he could stand, so I hoped it wouldn't be any trouble. The king had a shallow cut across his chest, and his hair was shorter by four inches on one side. Someone's sword had cut it off.

Charles thought that was incredibly funny. "Odd's fish. Better than *both* sides, if you catch my meaning," he said, and I couldn't argue with that.

I learned, then, that Lord Ashcombe had spotted my warning. He told me the king's escort had pulled up within a hundred yards of Barnham Wood when my first firework flashed behind them. For a moment, he'd thought it was lightning, until he realized there wasn't a cloud in the sky.

He'd called for a halt, waiting, frowning.

"Saw your second firework then," he said. "You were either celebrating or trying to warn someone. And I didn't think you were celebrating."

Lord Ashcombe had pulled the king from the carriage, and arranged his men on the ridge, the most defensible position he could see. "The Covenanters must have realized their ambush had failed. They came pouring from the trees and fired their volley. We shot back, and then they charged. You arrived soon after." He frowned. "Why *are* you here?"

I told him what had happened, what we'd discovered. When he read the letter I'd found in Domhnall Ardrey's desk, his face darkened, and he shouted for our reinforcements to return.

As for me, I was relieved. It was certain now that Lord Ashcombe couldn't be the "man in black" mentioned in the letter, and not merely because I didn't want him to be. He'd defended the king with the ferocity of a lion. This man was no traitor.

The king read the letter as Lord Ashcombe turned back to me. "Was Ardrey in the palace when you found this?" he asked.

"No," I said.

"Then I know where he is."

As the King's Men galloped up to the ridge, Lord Ashcombe barked out orders. "Ten of you with me. The rest see to the wounded." He turned to me. "Where's your horse?"

"We were attacked," I said. "She ran away."

He ordered one of the King's Men who'd relieved us to lend me his. As I waited, I said, "Could someone please look for Blossom?"

"There's no time for that," Lord Ashcombe said shortly.

"I know. I don't mean now. But . . . please." What had happened to Blossom was my fault. "She's hurt, and she's scared, and she's out there somewhere, all alone. I wouldn't have made it in time without her." I looked at the king. "Please."

Charles regarded me a moment, then nodded. He'd always held great affection for horses. "I'll send a man to search for her. But tomorrow. We have wounded to care for tonight."

Tom found Lightning, who'd stomped his way out of the circle near the end of the battle and was now calmly munching on shoots of grass in the field. One of the King's Men helped me up on his horse; he said his name was Chuff.

Chuff tilted his head a little so he could see me on his back. He snorted, pawing the earth, ears pricked in my direction. Then we were off.

We rode at full gallop back to Whitehall, His Majesty in the center. Lord Ashcombe had been right: My arm hurt now, throbbing with a vengeance. If I'd had the time, I'd have made some willow bark infusion, maybe even poppy. Instead, I had to make do by swallowing bitter willow powder dry.

For Lord Ashcombe was on the warpath. As we rode through Holbein Gate, he ordered six of his men to take the king and lock him in his quarters. "Let no one in," he said, his one eye burning. *"No one."*

Sally was there, waiting nervously by the stables. When she saw us, she nearly cried in relief. She sprinted toward us, dress flapping about her legs. Her look turned to horror as she saw the blood.

I had so much I wanted to tell her. But we didn't have time to explain. "Wounded are coming," I said. "Gather anyone you can. And find the king's surgeon."

Then we were riding again. Lord Ashcombe galloped ahead, and we followed him, all the way to Hatton Garden, a street near Clerkenwell Green.

We were going after the Scottish traitors.

We pulled up, four doors down from a house built of pink brick. "One man on each corner," he said quietly to the soldiers accompanying him. "No one escapes. Cut them down if you must, but I want them alive."

"Where are we?" Tom whispered to me.

I didn't know, but Lord Ashcombe heard him and answered. "Niall Ramsay's house. The man you saw with Domhnall Ardrey outside the palace." And presumably, the *N* who'd written the traitorous letter we'd found in Ardrey's quarters.

"Stay with the horses," Lord Ashcombe commanded.

His men began to spread out, two going round to cut off any runners from the back. Lord Ashcombe only got a few steps away.

Then Niall Ramsay's house exploded.

CHAPTER

THE WALLS BURST OUTWARD WITH

a terrible *whump*.

Brick, timber, and glass sprayed everywhere. Debris rained down on the road and the houses nearby. We ducked and covered our heads. The horses grunted and shied away in alarm.

I stared at the burning wreckage, mouth agape. Lord Ashcombe glanced at me—so did Tom—but I just shook my head. For once, an explosion wasn't my doing.

People rushed from their homes, panicked and stunned. "Fire! Fire!" someone shouted, and a chorus took up the echo.

"Water!" Lord Ashcombe commanded his men, and they ran to help the residents.

Niall Ramsay's house was gone. The entire face was blown away, chunks of pink brick littering the street. The back wall and part of the left side were still standing. Everything else was rubble.

The neighboring houses had taken the brunt of the blast. On the east, the whole side of the home next door had crumbled. The house to the west was pockmarked where the brick had peppered it, the roof starting to burn at the edge. Across the way looked the same, all the windows shattered.

Tom began tearing at the rubble, looking for injured, hoping to find survivors. I helped, grabbing the smaller bricks, while neighbors poured water over the flames, then ran back into their homes to refill their buckets from whatever stores they had. Others sprinted toward the closest wells, the King's Men alongside to assist.

An old woman staggered from the house on the right, dazed and bleeding from her temple. Tom hurried to help, leaving the wreckage behind. I would have followed, but a croaking voice stopped me.

"Christopher."

A man crawled through the rubble. He was burned so

badly that he barely looked human. I ran to him, hoping I could help, and in the chaos and confusion, it took me a moment to realize he'd called me by name.

He looked up at me, one eye stuck shut.

"Christopher," he said again.

This time, I made out the Scottish accent. And I realized who it was.

Domhnall Ardrey, Baron of Oxton. Covenanter.

Traitor.

I turned to call for Lord Ashcombe.

"Wait," Ardrey croaked. "I am not . . . your enemy."

The tone in his voice—desperate—stopped me.

I crouched beside him. "You tried to murder the king."

"No. Not . . . us. I am . . . a friend."

What was that supposed to mean? "You're a Covenanter." I paused. "Aren't you?"

He tried to answer but fell into a coughing fit. Finally, he just shook his head.

I frowned. If he wasn't a Covenanter . . . "Who are you?"

He looked me in the eye. "You have . . . a coin."

It took a moment for me to realize what he meant.

Then my stomach fell.

"You're a Templar," I whispered.

He nodded.

I knelt beside him. He was so terribly burned. "What happened here?"

He gasped for breath. "Knocked out . . . tied up. All . . . my brothers."

He motioned weakly behind him. There I saw a charred, knotted rope. It had burned enough to let the man free.

"This was . . . our chapter house," Ardrey said. "Brothers . . . gone. Templars . . . in London . . . finished. Betrayed."

Someone had betrayed the *Templars*. They'd tied them up and left them here to die in the explosion. It was a miracle Ardrey had even survived.

I was more confused than ever. "I found a letter," I said. "It claimed you were part of the plot to kill the king."

"Not . . . real. Lies."

"Then you helped save His Majesty," I said quietly. "I worked out your final puzzle."

He looked at me oddly. "What . . . puzzle?"

"In the Templar letters. The four you sent me."

He shook his head. "Not . . . us. We sent you . . . nothing."

I sat there, stunned, as the world spun around me.

The Templars . . . *hadn't* sent the letters?

But then . . . who . . . ?

All the blood drained from my face.

Because I knew who had sent the letters. I knew.

I'd been tricked right from the start.

A charred hand grabbed my wrist. "Your . . . enemy. You must . . . find . . . the priest."

"What priest?" I said. "Do you mean Father Bernard? He left Paris before we did. I don't know where he's gone."

"Find . . . the priest!" the man gasped.

Then Domhnall Ardrey, last of the London Knights Templar, died in my arms.

CHAPTER

BOOTS CRUNCHED THROUGH THE
rubble, approaching from behind.

"So," Lord Ashcombe said. "You found the traitor."

"He wasn't a traitor," I said quietly.

Lord Ashcombe frowned. "Explain."

"Ardrey told me so."

"The easiest thing in the world, to claim innocence."

Lord Ashcombe turned to go. I had to keep the Templars'
secret; I knew that. But I couldn't let this man take the blame
for treason.

"Look at his wrists."

Lord Ashcombe regarded me a moment. Then he bent down to examine the body.

"Ardrey was caught in the explosion," I said. "He's completely burned—except for one spot: his wrists. They weren't burned, because they were protected. By that."

I pointed to the charred, frayed rope farther back among the stones. Lord Ashcombe picked it up, brought it over. When he laid it against Ardrey's wrists, it matched the unburned parts perfectly.

He peered closer now, examining the skin. There was still an imprint of the rope in the flesh.

"He was bound when it happened," Lord Ashcombe said.

"That's what he told me," I said. "He was knocked out and brought here—he didn't know by whom—and left to die. The letter I found, in his quarters, at Whitehall . . . I was *meant* to find it. It was a fake. Everything was a fake."

My despair was overwhelming. I just wanted to lie down somewhere and never wake up again.

"It was all so clever," I said. "The letter pins the blame on Domhnall Ardrey and Niall Ramsay. They die here, with God knows how many others lost under the rubble. The letter also names a man in black—and of course that's supposed to be you; who else could it be? You were to die, too, alongside His Majesty, in the ambush at Barnham Wood. All of you then blamed as traitors. All of you dead, unable to speak in your own defense."

"And the real traitor goes free," Lord Ashcombe said.

I nodded. "I'm sorry."

"For what?"

For everything. "The man in black. The letter. I'm sorry I ever thought it was you."

Lord Ashcombe waved my apology away. He stood and called two of the King's Men.

"Take the body to Whitehall. This, too." He dropped the frayed rope on Ardrey's chest. "No one touches anything until I return."

They began to carry the corpse. "Come," Lord Ashcombe said to me. "There's still work to be done."

I sat there for a moment, just a moment longer.

Then I pushed myself to my feet and followed the King's Warden into the fire.

MARCH 6–7, 1666

The instruments of darkness tell us truths,

Win us with honest trifles, to betray us

In deepest consequence.

CHAPTER
53

IT WAS THE EARLY HOURS OF THE
morning before we returned to the palace. Tom wobbled,
half-asleep in his saddle, covered in soot, dirt, and blood. I
steadied him as we rode, feeling much the same.

We dismounted at the stable. "Leave the horses to the
groom," Lord Ashcombe said. "See to your wounds."

His command reminded me of the groom we'd caught
earlier, the secret Covenanter. I would have asked what happened to him, but I was simply too tired to care. It could wait.

We trudged over to the tiltyard, where the wounded
from the ambush at Barnham Wood had been arriving all
night, carried on horseback. Many of the King's Men had

died from their injuries; the bodies lay untended near the jousting rail. The rest had largely been cared for, which was a blessing. I don't think I could have borne any more screaming.

Men and women worked under the soft light of the torches staked around the yard. From the blood that drenched their aprons, at least two were surgeons. Master Kirby walked among them, offering remedies and poultices to cover gashes against infection.

He'd already prepared an infusion of poppy; I could smell the cauldron from here. It had allowed the worst of the wounded to doze, to steal a few hours of peace before they awoke once more to agony.

Sally was there, too, gathering rags, bandaging wounds, administering potions, offering comfort. Her dress, like everything else, was covered in blood and dirt, ruined. Her cheeks were smudged. Her hair, tied back, had come loose on one side, auburn curls tumbling past her ear. She pushed them away absently as she worked. And, in the glow of the torches, she was the most beautiful thing I'd ever seen.

She saw us and hurried over. "Are you all right?"

We lowered ourselves to the ground and nodded, too tired to speak.

"I have to tend to the others," she said. "There's an order to seeing the wounded."

She squeezed our hands, then hurried back to finish dressing wounds. Wings flapped at me, salt-and-pepper speckled, as Bridget came to land on my lap. I'd thought she was locked in my quarters; had Sally let her out? I'd have figured she was too busy to bother.

As glad as I was to see Bridget, I was too tired to even stroke her feathers. I just let her walk all over me, fly to my shoulder, my head, then back again to my feet.

Master Kirby passed by, a cup of poppy in his hands, and glanced at the pigeon. When he finally noticed whom Bridget was climbing over, he stopped and stared.

I stood, joints cracking. "Do you need my help, Master?"

He looked me up and down, saw the cut on my arm, the slump in my bones, the muck and the filth.

"Busy day for everyone, it seems." When I didn't answer, he waved me back to the ground. "Not tonight, Rowe," he said softly. I sat as ordered, gladly.

The few King's Men who'd suffered only cuts and scrapes had dressed their own wounds, so Tom and I were the last to be seen. The surgeon looked us over, put a half dozen stitches in Tom's leg, and three in my arm. He offered us the poppy. Tom took it; I didn't.

Sally tended to Tom while the surgeon worked on me. She wiped his wounds clean with a damp cloth as he lay in the dirt, drifting off to sleep. When the surgeon left, and Sally had finished, she nudged him. "Time for bed."

Tom curled up on the ground. "M'already in bed."

She laughed. "Go on, now, go on."

"Mn. Wait for Christophmrr."

"I'll be fine," I said. He would ache like the devil in the morning. I couldn't imagine how much worse it would be if he slept all night on the ground. I poked him until he sat up. "Go inside. Take Bridget. Come on, if you fall asleep, I won't be able to carry you."

"Mnngln," he grumbled, but he staggered off to our quarters, Bridget cupped in his hands, bumping into the wall along the way.

"I should go, too," I said.

"You can't sleep like that," Sally said. "Let me look at you."

She tried to help me take off my shirt, but my arm hurt too much to lift. "Just cut it off," I said. "It's ruined, anyway."

Sally used a knife to split it from collar to hem, then drew a breath when she saw the damage underneath. My arm was bloody where I'd been cut, flesh bound together by the stitches, and I had scrapes all over my shoulder, chest, and back. Everything else was bruised and swollen, angry red splotches covering my skin.

"Christopher," Sally said, dismayed.

"At least no one shot me this time."

"What happened out there?"

I bowed my head and sighed. "I fell off a horse."

She leaned in close, dabbing my skin with cold water. It helped dull the pain. A little.

"Everyone keeps talking about you to me," I said.

"Oh?" Sally wiped the dirt away. After a moment, she asked, "What are they saying?"

I didn't answer. She cleaned me up and wrapped a bandage around my arm.

"You should take the poppy," she said.

"I'll be fine."

She looked into my eyes, searching. Then she leaned in and kissed me softly on the cheek.

Sally stayed there, her head against mine, her breath warm on my neck. I wanted her to stay like that forever.

One of the King's Men woke and moaned. She went to him. I trudged up to bed.

CHAPTER

54

I SLEPT ALMOST THE ENTIRE DAY. I
kept waking, body throbbing with pain, then falling back
for a few more fitful minutes. Tom did the same. Eventually we gave up and just lay there, watching the boats float
along the Thames, playing with Bridget, and talking across
the room about nothing at all.

"Should we be doing something?" Tom said.

At that moment, I honestly didn't care. "If they want
us, they know where we are."

I told Tom everything that had happened yesterday. Sally, who'd stayed up all night helping care for the
wounded, came by to see us, exhausted, and I told her every-

thing, too. They were horrified at the death of the Templars, and the collapse of the London chapter, and just how close our enemy had come to blaming everything on them, and Lord Ashcombe, too. We didn't talk about who the enemy was. They already knew.

After a short nap in our chair, Sally returned to the tiltyard, leaving Tom and me once again in idle conversation. Until the evening, when we were roused by a knock on the door.

I answered it, every muscle howling at being asked to move. It was a servant with a folded note. "You're requested, sir," he said, and left.

I'd just about opened the note when I saw the name on it. The servant had mistaken me for Tom. "It's for you."

Tom was still in bed. When he read the note, he sat up, eyes widening.

"What is it?" I said.

"Oh . . . I'm supposed to give a report on yesterday. All the fighting. To the captain of the Horse Guards."

Wincing, he got dressed, stuffing the note in his pocket. My heart sank. I'd have known he was lying, even if he hadn't made it so obvious. He looked so sad again.

And suddenly I knew. I knew what Lord Ashcombe had offered him. What gift the king had given.

You've changed, Dorothy had said when I'd returned to Blackthorn. Maybe she'd been right. But I wasn't the only one.

Tom had changed, too.

Not in the most important ways. Inside, he was still the kind, gentle, innocent best friend I'd met on Clerkenwell Green, all those years ago. But being out from under his father's thumb, learning the sword, finding his courage when the people he loved were in danger, it had changed him, the same as it had me.

He was still the nervous sort—I don't think he'd ever lose that—but he was growing into a great man. When we were smaller—or younger, really; had Tom ever been small?—he'd dreamed of becoming a knight. He was, at least, now a soldier. Of course Lord Ashcombe would see that. And of course he'd tell His Majesty.

It's hard to say no to a king, Tom had said.

And so I finally understood: He was leaving.

Tom finished buttoning his doublet.

"If there's something you want to tell me," I said, "you can. I won't be cross, or upset."

"What's there to tell?" He wouldn't meet my eyes. "I'll be back soon."

He left, limping badly on his wounded leg. I sat on the

bed, despairing. Tom was the only person I had left from when I'd lived with Master Benedict.

I called to my master in heaven. *What do I do?*

Wait for him, Master Benedict said.

It was good advice. But if Tom was leaving . . . I didn't know how I'd get by with him not around.

So I did something I'd never done before: I ignored what Master Benedict said. I threw on some clothes as quick as I could and snuck after my friend.

His path away from our room told the tale. The Horse Guards were quartered beside the tiltyard, which was to the west. Tom limped through the palace toward the south. When he entered the Privy Garden, I hurried up the stairs.

There was a balcony over the Stone Gallery. I crouched there, hidden behind the balustrade, peeking down into the garden. Tom approached the men he'd been called to meet.

Lord Ashcombe, Walsingham, and the king.

"Thomas!" The king greeted him warmly. "My brother in arms. Some fight last night, eh?"

Tom flushed, pleased. "Yes, Your Majesty."

"The way you and Christopher rode in on that horse—I thought it was Saint George himself, come to slay the dragon. Richard had already told me the men speak your name with respect. You couldn't have proved yourself better last night. To them, and to me, as well."

I don't think I'd ever seen Tom more proud—or more tormented.

"So, what do you say?" the king continued. "Will you accept my offer and join my army?"

I laid my head against the rail. I'd guessed right. How I wished I hadn't.

Tom struggled for an answer. "May I ask a question, sire?"

"Anything."

"What would it mean if I accepted?"

Lord Ashcombe answered him. "You'll leave immediately for the camp at Gravesend. You'll train for a year. Then His Majesty will request you back, where you'll become part of the King's Men, under my command."

"And . . . what about Christopher? Could he come with me?"

Lord Ashcombe regarded him. "He's free to join," he said slowly, "but you're aware His Majesty has other plans for him. Besides, I think you know: Christopher isn't meant for a soldier's life."

"No," Tom said miserably. "In that case . . ." He struggled to get the words out. "I'm sorry, sire. I can't."

My heart leaped.

Tom turned to Lord Ashcombe, pleading. "Christopher *needs* me. You know what he's like. Always getting into trouble. It's not *always* his fault . . . well, not *most* of the time . . . well, not some of the time. But he'd have died in Saint Paul's without me. I can't abandon him."

And now my heart broke. Tom looked so stricken.

"Come here, child," Charles said, and he clasped Tom's hands.

"You're not angry?" Tom said.

"Of course not. I know what such friendship is worth." The king nodded toward Lord Ashcombe. "Christopher is blessed to have you. As am I."

"Does this mean I won't . . . ?" Tom bit his lip.

"Go on. Ask."

"Er . . . could I still train with Sir William Leech?"

"That monster? Odd's fish. I think I still have the bruises he gave me when I was your age." The king looked amused. "What do you say, gentlemen? Should I permit it?"

"My apprentice," Walsingham said softly, "does appear to find himself in places he shouldn't. A well-trained guard would be prudent."

Lord Ashcombe shrugged. "If Your Majesty wills it."

"My Majesty does. Go on, Thomas, rest. All is well."

Tom bowed and left. They watched him limp away.

"What an extraordinary young man," Charles said, wistful. "Come, friends. Let's drink the night away."

Lord Ashcombe and Charles turned to leave. Time for me to sneak out of here, too.

Walsingham stopped us all. "With your permission, sire, I'll join you in a moment. There is a matter I must attend to."

"Oh? Very well. Hurry, then."

The king left with Lord Ashcombe. Walsingham waited until they'd disappeared. Then he spoke. It was the first time I'd ever heard him raise his voice above a murmur.

"Loyalty like that is so rare." His words carried through the garden. "Don't you think?"

I froze.

The spymaster waited, his back to me.

Finally, sheepishly, I stood. "Yes, my lord."

He turned and looked up. "I dislike speaking this way."

I went downstairs, burning red. "Sorry, my lord."

"For what?" Walsingham said.

"Well . . . for spying on you. And His Majesty."

"That's your job."

"I thought it was to spy on *other* people."

He shrugged. "Do as you need. If there is trouble, I will sort it out."

The man continued to surprise me. But there *was* something else I was sorry for. Something that left me deeply ashamed.

"I failed you," I said.

"How?"

"The king was nearly killed because of me. I was duped."

"So were we all. As I told you before, your job is to keep us informed. The decision—the responsibility—is ours."

"But—"

"Your efforts to accept blame are tedious," the spymaster said, and that was the end of that. "On to other matters. I have examined Ardrey's corpse. I agree with your conclusion. He was bound at the time of the explosion. So we may be certain: A traitor still walks among us."

"What about the groom who tried to stop me?" I said.

"He confesses to being a Covenanter. He denies knowledge of other conspirators. He claims instructions came only by letter."

"Do you believe him?"

"He was questioned most vigorously. Could he withstand such pressure?" Walsingham shrugged. "There are men who can. I think, however, he is not one of them. I consider his statements credible. He is *a* traitor, but not *the* traitor."

"Do you know who that is?" I said.

"No. Do you?"

That took me aback a little. "In the palace? I'm sorry, my lord, I don't know enough people here to say."

"It appears none of us do. I like these flowers."

He stared down at some early blooming hyacinths.

I didn't think I'd ever get used to the spymaster's ways. "Er . . . yes, my lord. I also . . . I wanted to talk to you about the messages I was sent. With the puzzles."

He nodded. "So we should."

"I think . . . I think they were sent by the Raven."

"I thought the Raven was dead."

His words were less a question, more a challenge for me to explain.

"*Rémi* is dead," I said. "Simon Chastellain is certain of that. But we never knew for a fact that the Raven was Rémi. It could have been someone else pulling the strings."

"That is possibility, not proof."

"It explains the attack on Simon, though. Why would Covenanters care about a French vicomte? We explained it away as him being a friend of mine, but really, that was just us twisting the evidence to fit our theory." Which was exactly what Walsingham had warned me not to do. "It had to be the Raven who sent that assassin. Only he had a grudge against both of us."

"A stronger possibility," the spymaster agreed. "Yet still not proof."

Perhaps not—but this was. "Only the Raven could have sent me the letters."

Walsingham was still staring at the hyacinths. "Justify your claim."

"The riddles, the puzzles," I said. "They weren't just sent *to* me. They were *about* me. The first one told me to remember Paris. The second was based on Alberti's disk, which Master Benedict had taught me to use. The third required me to recognize that 'swan' meant arsenic, and find its symbol— again, things Master Benedict taught me as an apothecary and alchemist. And the fourth . . . it was handed to me by people in costume, telling the story of what's happened to me since my master died. The archangel, the plague doctor, the—" I left out the Templar. "The White Lady.

"They had to know me," I continued, "and know my master, too. When I was in Paris, at Maison Chastellain,

I spoke of what happened with the Cult of the Archangel and Melchior. Rémi heard it. And, of course, he knew of my hunt for the old Templar treasure, and the puzzles I'd found. If he told the Raven—the *real* Raven . . .

"What's more, in the Raven's letter to me, he said he knew Master Benedict, years ago. That my master had been a thorn in his side. Only the Raven could know all of my past."

I'd thought the letters were being sent to me by the Templars. The riddles were just like the ones I'd found in Paris, so I'd made assumptions. Jumped to conclusions. Again. Even though I knew better.

In the end, it was all just trickery on the Raven's part. He'd played me for a fool.

Walsingham considered what I'd said. "The White Lady lived in the wilds of Devonshire," he noted. "How could the Raven know that?"

"I sent letters to Simon," I said, "telling him about it. He never got them, which is why he came to London looking for me. We both assumed the letters had just been lost in this winter's terrible storms.

"But what if they weren't? What if the letters never arrived *because they'd been intercepted*?"

"By the Raven," Walsingham said.

"Yes."

He stood there, silent.

"I really think—"

The spymaster raised a hand. "Your logic is sound. I agree."

I slumped in relief. I hadn't realized just how badly I'd needed to be believed.

"There is another incident," Walsingham said, "of which you are unaware. The attack on His Majesty was not the only event of yesterday."

He finally turned away from the flowers. "Late last night," he said, "while the party continued at Berkshire House, the vault in the secret passage was robbed."

"*What?*" That didn't make sense. "Sally didn't say she collected the guards from underground."

"She didn't. Those soldiers died at their post. We found them shot in the back, with crossbow bolts."

I was stunned. "How could this happen?"

"From what I've been able to gather," Walsingham said, "I believe someone at the party went down to the cellar and opened the secret entrance. This had to be planned—for when the King's Men confronted the intruder, they were shot from behind."

"The conspirators must have entered from Saint James's Park. Crossbows were used, I suspect, so there would be no noise of gunshots. The locks were then picked, and the jewelry looted, carried back out through the park. I imagine the ringleader even returned to the party.

"Covenanters would not have split their forces to attack the king *and* rob him at the same time. This was the work of someone else: a man who knew the ambush would take place, but cared nothing for its outcome. All he wanted was the money."

"The Raven," I whispered.

"Combined with the personal knowledge of you, and the letters you were sent? It is the only reasonable conclusion."

Now it all made sense. The Raven had been working with the Covenanters all along. He'd sent me the letters, knowing I'd think they were from the Templars, so I'd follow the clues, expose the plot against the king, and help get Charles out of the palace so he could be ambushed.

But as the Raven had used me, so had he used the Covenanters. Their struggle didn't mean anything to him. Instead, he'd exploited the fact that most of the King's Men were away so he could rob the secret treasury.

And at the same time, he'd somehow discovered who was in the London chapter of the Knights Templar. He'd lured Domhnall Ardrey to the Banqueting House so I would see him and think him an enemy. Then he'd planted the fake letter in Ardrey's desk to pin the blame on the baron, before blowing up their chapter house, killing them all.

Revenge on me, for stealing his treasure in Paris. Revenge on the Templars. And he'd made himself richer in the process. How he must be laughing at me.

"What do we do now?" I said miserably.

"All we can," Walsingham said. "You investigate at your end. I shall investigate at mine. If you need assistance, let me know. I will do the same."

He regarded me. "You may not accept it, but my assessment remains. I consider your performance satisfactory."

He returned his gaze to the flowers. I left him, alone, in the garden.

I bumped into Tom entering our rooms.

"I was just about to go looking for you," he said. "Where'd you go?"

"Out for a walk," I said.

"You're supposed to be resting."

"So are you. But you're still limping around."

And of course he was—because he was looking for me. I gave him a giant hug.

"What's that for?" he said, puzzled.

"Nothing."

His eyes narrowed. "Where *did* you go, exactly?"

"I told you. For a walk."

"And did this walk take you anywhere near the Privy Garden?"

" . . . Maybe."

"Christopher!" he said, shocked. "You spied on me!"

"As Lord Walsingham noted, that *is* my job now."

He shook a fist at me and sputtered. "Odd's fish!"

"I'm sorry," I said, and the rest came rushing out. "It's just . . . you were so *sad*. And I didn't know why, and you wouldn't tell me—you even lied about it. And then, when you got that note, I finally realized what it might be. I just . . . I didn't want you to leave. You're the best friend I could ever have. I don't know what I'd do without you."

"Well . . ." He flushed, embarrassed. "You could start by not setting things on fire."

"I'll have you know—" I said.

"Oh, here we go."

"—*my* fireworks saved the king. The king! How many people can say that? I'll tell you. One. Me."

"Oh *no*."

"In fact . . . I should open a new line. Blackthorn's Blasters! Guaranteed to maintain a monarch! Or your penny back."

Tom buried his face in his hands. "Why, Lord? Why me?"

I turned serious for a moment. "I really am grateful, Tom. You've saved my life more times than I can count."

"Which is a problem in itself," he pointed out. "But you've saved my life, too, remember? During the plague, and in Devonshire. We're even."

"We're not even close to even."

"Doesn't matter. That's my job," he said. "I promise you, Christopher, if the Raven wants to get you, he'll have to step over my dead body to do it."

And then the most terrible chill washed over me, as if a ghost had passed through the room. I shuddered. "Don't say that."

For I had the feeling his words would come true.

CHAPTER

55

I FELT A LITTLE BETTER THE NEXT day. With things resolved with Tom, and no one blaming me for what had happened—even if I still blamed myself—our problems didn't seem quite so grim. Despite the fact that I still hurt all over.

Everyone agreed now: Not only was the Raven still alive, he was here in London.

Walsingham believed someone at the party at Berkshire House had distracted the guards to allow the secret vault to be looted. Was that the Raven? It was strange to think that he might have been so close.

Then another thing occurred to me. Simon had said the

Raven specialized in pretending to be someone else. So if the Raven actually was at that party . . .

My stomach fluttered. *This might be something we could discover. Find out who was there—and investigate them. If we could find a false identity . . . someone who didn't belong . . .* I resolved to bring it up with the spymaster.

Something else happened that made me feel better, too. Late that morning, one of the King's Men knocked on our door. I figured he was here for Tom, until I recognized him. It was the man who'd lent me his warhorse, Chuff.

He'd found Blossom!

I limped along with him to the stables. Sure enough, there was the old girl, safe in her stall. She nickered, and I held her while she chewed on the back of my coat. "Where did you find her?"

"On a farm near Parsons Green," the King's Man said. "She wandered in among the cows. Farmer said she was making friends."

"Of course she was. She's a sweet old thing. Aren't you, girl?"

I was so happy, I gave the King's Man a pound for his troubles, which made his eyes bulge. He left, delighted, as I looked Blossom over. She had a nasty gouge on her chest, where the rope strung across the road had hit her, and other bruises and cuts from the fall. But the groom—a new man, thankfully—said there was no permanent damage, and she'd heal well enough, given time. I stayed with her a bit, brushing her coat and sneaking her sugar from the vial in my apothecary sash, while she bobbed her head at Bridget, who marched along the stall door.

In the meantime, Isaac was supposed to be reading Master Benedict's journals. When Sally returned to the palace, finally rested from a good night's sleep, I suggested we all go check on him, and on Simon, too. We'd need to tell them both about the Raven, anyway.

As Blossom needed rest, I suggested we take different horses. Sally insisted we use a carriage. "If it wasn't for Isaac," she said, "I wouldn't even let you two out."

Tom and I saluted her. "Yes, ma'am," we said, and she glared at us.

Bridget flew off into the sky as soon as the carriage started rolling, heading home to Blackthorn, no doubt. She'd have to wait for us there, because I wanted to see Isaac first, to find out what he'd discovered.

We found him in his shop, leaning heavily on a stool, a mop in hand and a soapy bucket near the counter. Judging from the water smeared on the floor, he'd managed only a few swipes before sitting back down. He tried to hide it, but he looked in terrible pain.

Sally, already in a bit of a mood due to our casual disregard for our injuries, narrowed her eyes. "What were you doing?"

"Just tidying up a little," Isaac said.

"I told you I'd come by and help."

"I can do it."

"We'll all help," I said, and then Sally finally lost her temper.

"Sit," she ordered, pointing at each one of us in turn. "You, too. And you—give me the mop." She shook her head. *"Boys."*

"Perhaps we should let her be," Isaac mused.

Tom and I helped him up the stairs and, in his quarters, told him everything that had happened.

He shook his head in regret. "Too much to hope the Raven was gone, I suppose. At least you all survived."

"Have you found anything in Master Benedict's journals?" I asked.

"I'm sorry, no. Not that I've got very far. That's something I need to talk to you about." He sighed. "It won't come as any secret to you that I'm not well."

My blood went cold. Isaac saw the look on my face and patted my arm.

"I'm not ill," he said, "in the 'my time is drawing near' sense. But I am in pain. It's arthritis. I've had it for years. Since the plague, it's been worse than ever."

"I can help with that," I said, and he nodded.

"Benedict used to make me a potion. It would be a great kindness if you could find his recipe."

I stood. "I'll go look for it right now."

"Wait." He bade me sit again. "I need to ask something of you. I told you before I locked myself away that I'd made a terrible mistake. In my desire to keep the underground library a secret, I never took on an apprentice. It's clear, now, that I must. I need help."

"Of course," I said. "I'll do what I can—"

"We both will—" Tom said.

"No." Isaac waved us off. "Christopher, you would have made a wonderful librarian. But to care for such a collection takes an immense amount of time. You already have two masters. I doubt, especially after this week's events, that the king will willingly let you go.

"And to stop you from pursuing life as an apothecary? Never. I know how much it means to you, and how much it meant to Benedict, too. He didn't just leave you the shop because he loved you. He knew you would carry on his legacy with pride.

"As for you, Tom," Isaac continued, "I trust you as I do Christopher. But do you really want a lifetime of nothing but books?"

Tom shook his head.

"So there you are. Nonetheless, I must have help. I believe God has provided, through you. What do you think about Sally?"

Tom and I looked at each other, surprised. I could hear her downstairs, singing. "To take over the library?" I said. "I think it's a brilliant idea."

"Are you certain? She'd have to learn many languages. She knows no Greek, and her Latin is nearly nonexistent."

"They don't teach such things to the girls at Cripplegate. But her French is excellent, better than mine. She'll learn, I'm sure of it."

"But will she want to do it?" Isaac worried. "It's a tremendous amount of work, and responsibility. As the king's ward, she has a life of leisure ahead of her."

"She doesn't want that. See the way she speaks to us walking wounded? She wants to be useful. I'm telling you, ask her."

He called down to her. "Sally?"

She stopped singing and came up. "Did you need something?"

"As a matter of fact, yes," Isaac said. "Would you be willing to spend more time here, with me? I could use your help in the library. And perhaps you'd be interested in studying some Latin, or Greek?"

Her jaw dropped. "You mean it? Yes! Oh, thank you!"

She hugged him. I'd never seen anyone so happy about learning Greek.

"I'll come whenever you like," she said. "Every day." And she went back downstairs, singing a merry tune.

"That was easier than I'd hoped," Isaac said. "Though there is one thing that worries me."

"What's that?" I said.

"At some point, Sally is likely to want to marry, and have a family. Any suitor would have to be someone of impeccable trust." He looked at me speculatively. "I don't suppose you've ever considered . . . ?"

Tom fell off his chair, laughing.

While Sally remained to look after Isaac, Tom and I took the carriage to Blackthorn, on the hunt for Master Benedict's arthritis remedy. Henri was in the shop as usual, snoozing on the stool behind the counter. Upstairs, we heard a pair of voices singing an old French folk song, neither one particularly well.

In my bedroom, we found Simon, lying on his stomach, and Dr. Kemp, sitting beside him, chair leaning against the wall. On the bed between them was Master Benedict's chessboard, a game in progress.

It didn't look like they'd got very far. Both were drinking, a squat-bottomed bottle between them, the source of the brandy in their cups—and, no doubt, the song in their hearts, as well.

"Ah!" Dr. Kemp said as we squeezed our way through the book stacks. His eyes were a little red from drink. "The boy apothecary returns."

"I hope you don't mind, Christopher," Simon said. "The doctor here spotted the board in your workshop and offered me a game."

"Not at all," I said. "Who's winning?"

"I am," they said in unison, and laughed.

"I hope you don't mind us raiding your stash of brandy, either," Dr. Kemp said.

"That's not mine," I said, puzzled.

Too late, I saw Simon put a finger to his lips. Dr. Kemp saw it, too.

"What?" he said to Simon, with an outrage I wasn't entirely sure was genuine. "You said the boy ordered it. For medicinal purposes!"

"It *is* medicinal," Simon said casually. "Boredom kills."

"Blaming it on a child. I should have known better than to trust a Frenchman." He stood, snatching the bottle away. "I'm taking this as punishment." He winked at me as he left.

Simon shouted after him. "You're taking it because you're a *quack*—oh! Ow."

"Lie down," I said.

"I keep forgetting my back," Simon said. "Then I move, and it reminds me. Would you ask Henri to return to my room at the inn? I have a few more bottles of brandy left. I finally understand why my uncle loved the stuff so. Helps the pain, you know."

"Sure." I lifted the chessboard from the bed and balanced it on a stack of books, careful not to move the pieces. "I'm sorry we haven't been around much. It's been mad, the last few days." I sighed. "There's something I have to tell you. The Raven isn't dead."

Simon listened, shocked, as I recounted most of what had happened. I kept my new apprenticeship to the spymaster a secret, as ordered, and said nothing about the Templars. But by the time I was finished, he was furious.

He tried to get out of bed. Tom and I pushed him down until he calmed.

He cursed in French. "I'm sorry, Christopher. I truly thought he was ended."

As disappointed as I was, the truth hadn't cut me so deeply. Because, in my heart, I'd never really believed the Raven was dead.

"What happens now?" Simon said, eyes hard. He was thinking once again of revenge.

"His Majesty has promised me help. In the meantime, we'll keep looking."

"You have my help as well. Anything you need. As soon as that quack lets me out of this bed."

I looked over at the window. It was open at the bottom, allowing fresh air in. "Did Bridget come?"

"Yes," Simon said. "An hour ago, or so. She pecked at the window, but by the time I dragged myself over to open it, she'd flown away."

I wondered if she'd gone up to the roof when she

couldn't get inside. That was where she'd once lived, before the Cult of the Archangel had destroyed our pigeon coop. "You mind checking for her?" I asked Tom. "I have to find Isaac's arthritis recipe."

Dutifully, Tom climbed up through the roof hatch in the hallway while I went down to the workshop to hunt through Master Benedict's notes. It didn't take long to find the correct paper. I remembered the formula, and even spotted the comment Master Benedict had written in the margin.

For I—twice daily.

I sent Henri to get Simon another bottle of brandy, as he'd requested, then pulled the ingredients together for my master's recipe and began to work. Tom came down the stairs, pigeonless.

"Nothing?" I said.

He shrugged. I shook my head. Bridget had been behaving so oddly since we'd returned, I didn't think too much of it. I assumed that, after we hadn't arrived at Blackthorn, she'd gone looking for me.

I was wrong.

I'd just finished Isaac's potion when I heard the door to

the shop open. I went out front to see a small boy of about nine poking his head in. "This Blackwell apothecary?"

"Blackthorn," I said.

"Right, that's it." The boy stepped in, gingerly holding a package wrapped in burlap. "Looking for Christopher. Man said you'd give me a penny if I delivered this. Careful. He said not to turn it over."

I fished a penny from my coin purse and traded it for the package. "What man?"

"Dunno. A right proper gentleman, he was, though." The boy tipped his cap and hurried out.

I pulled the burlap open. Inside was a simple box of unvarnished oak, the top fastened with a pair of latches. I could hear something sloshing around within. I unhooked the latches and opened the lid.

The smell was the first thing that hit me. Hot, thick, coppery.

Blood.

And so did I find blood inside. A pool of it, half an inch thick, at the bottom of the box. And there, in the middle, wrapped round with cord, was my pigeon.

"BRIDGET!" I screamed. "NO!"

I pulled her out, box falling from my hands. It hit the

floor, breaking apart at the hinges. Blood splashed on my boots, my hose, staining them scarlet and warm.

No, my mind kept shouting, over and over. *No no no no no no*

No.

She cooed.

Bridget, cupped in my hands, opened her eyes, and turned her head to look at me. Her feathers were soaked in blood.

She's alive! my mind howled. *She's alive,* I thought, a prayer.

Tom, who'd come limping when I screamed, stared in horror at the bloody bird in my palms.

"Get water. Water!" I shouted.

He ran into the workshop, came back with a giant bucket. I saw blood on his thigh. I wondered madly how he'd gotten blood from the box on him when he was in the workshop, before I realized that, in his hurry, he'd torn the stitches holding the wound together on his leg.

He scooped handfuls of water from the pail and let it rain on Bridget. She didn't even have enough energy to shake her head at the drops. I held her, bloody water running down my wrists, until most of it was gone. Then I cut the cord and turned her over, looking desperately for the wound in her little body.

Where is it? Where is it?

Master Benedict came then. *Calm, child. Think. Think of the blood.*

Think of the *blood?* Why would he say that? Didn't he know I couldn't think of anything else? There was so *much* of it, it was *all over the place—*

I stopped.

The blood. So much.

Too much. There had to be a pint of it, splashed all over my floorboards, staining my clothes. It couldn't have come from a pigeon.

Freed from her bonds, Bridget flopped about in my hands, righting herself. She shook her feathers out as Tom continued raining water over her, washing the rest of the red away. She spread her wings, flapped them weakly, once, twice. Then she walked up my arm until she was nestled in the crook of my elbow.

She was all right. She was going to be all right. Tears came hot to my eyes, and I blinked them away.

"Christopher."

Tom lifted the broken box from the floor. Inside the

lid, a pair of brass clamps held a letter. It was spotted with blood, crimson drips where the liquid had splashed when I'd dropped it.

There was another spot of red on it, too. A simple circle of wax, sealing it shut.

Cradling Bridget in my arms, I plucked the letter out and cracked the seal. The message inside was written in the same hand as all the letters I'd received, the letters I'd foolishly thought had come from the Templars. But this message offered no riddles, and no puzzle.

My dear Christopher,

Look what I found in the street. You should be more careful with your things. You wouldn't want to lose them.

With anticipation,
The Raven

A FEW MATTERS OF HISTORICAL NOTE

A friend of Charles II once wrote a poem about him. As the story goes, the poem was pinned to the door of the king's bedroom, for all to read:

> *Here lies our sovereign lord and king,*
> *Whose word no man relies on;*
> *He never says a foolish thing,*
> *Nor ever does a wise one.*

As usual, Charles responded with good humor, saying, "This is very true, for my words are my own, but my actions are my ministers'." And this more or less sums up his reputation: good-natured, intelligent, and funny—and also lazy, slippery, and ineffective.

There is some truth to these charges. Charles, the Merry Monarch, was one of the most popular kings of England, beloved by just about everyone—with some notable exceptions, as we have seen. Yet unlike more famous rulers such as Henry VIII or Elizabeth I, Charles was something of an underachiever.

His character was shaped by incredible events. By all accounts, he was a happy, sweet-natured, affectionate young boy. Then his life was overturned by rebellion. He saw his first battle at the age of twelve, eventually going on to fight in them himself until the Royalist armies were defeated and he was forced to flee England. (An extraordinary adventure during which he hid from enemy troops in an oak tree, stained his skin with walnut juice as a disguise, and pretended to be a servant—and an incompetent one, at that. It was a story Charles never tired of telling.)

When his father was executed, Charles was heartbroken. He spent the next eight years moving from country to country in exile. After he was finally restored to his throne, he was determined never to lose it again. Every decision was made according to whether it would strengthen or weaken his position. So, as noted, he was not above breaking oaths when necessary.

He did also give an impression of laziness, though this wasn't entirely true. Certainly, he enjoyed his leisure time to the point of self-indulgence, and he despised endless business meetings (though who can fault him for that? I can't stand them, either). But he worked harder than he let on. Many times he rose early, reading the day's missives in private, where no one could see him. So he was much more informed than his detractors gave him credit for.

Whatever his failings, in the end, his people loved him. While not the most accomplished king, he was a kind one, generous and forgiving, never cruel. He supported education and discovery, giving his patronage to found the Royal Society, the UK's national academy of sciences. He was brave in battle, a skilled swordsman and horseman, and, unlike many rulers, he cared genuinely for his countrymen.

During the Great Fire that devastated London in September 1666, Charles rode among his people, coordinating their efforts and organizing supplies to help them, rewarding the most heroic of firefighters by handing them gold guineas. And in the aftermath, he rebuilt London quickly, hiring genius architect Christopher Wren to return the city to glory. All in all, not a bad legacy, I think.

Speaking of fire, sadly, it would end up destroying much of London's heritage over the years. Unlike Christopher, Tom, and Sally's adventure in Paris, almost none of the locations they visit this time are still standing. Old St. Paul's Cathedral was lost to the Great Fire; the church that stands there now was rebuilt in its entirety (designed by the aforementioned Christopher Wren).

The Palace of Whitehall also burned down, in 1698, when a servant accidentally hung wet linen around a charcoal brazier to dry. Flames spread quickly through the complex, destroying almost everything except a few buildings, the Holbein Gate, and the Banqueting House—which was saved, once again, by Christopher Wren, then the King's Surveyor of Works, who bricked up the main window so fire couldn't spread through it.

Today, the only place remaining from this adventure is the Banqueting House. It's still there, the final remnant of a line of famous kings, and you can go and visit it (and rent it out for an event, if you like). You can even still see Rubens's magnificent paintings on the ceiling. Good thing Christopher didn't tear them down.

ACKNOWLEDGMENTS

It's my privilege to have so many talented folks helping put these books together. I'd like to say thank you to the following:

To Liesa Abrams and Suri Rosen, both of whom offered insights that made this story immeasurably better.

To Valerie Garfield, Jon Anderson, Christina Solazzo, Julie Doebler, Karin Paprocki, Hilary Zarycky, Brian Luster, Daphne Tagg, Christina Pecorale, Michelle Leo, Lauren Carr, Caitlin Sweeny, Anna Jarzab, Victor Iannone, Gary Urda, Emily Hutton, Stephanie Voros, Anna Parsons, and Kara Sargent at Aladdin.

To Kevin Hanson, Felicia Quon, Arden Hagedorn, Laura

MacDonald, Shara Alexa, and Rita Silva at Simon & Schuster Canada.

To Dan Lazar, Cecilia de la Campa, Torie Doherty-Munro, and James Munro at Writers House.

To the publishers around the world who have embraced the Blackthorn Key series.

And, as always, to you, dear reader: Thank you for joining Christopher on this adventure. One more to go . . .